Henri Dauge

A fair philosopher

Henri Dauge

A fair philosopher

ISBN/EAN: 9783743303201

Manufactured in Europe, USA, Canada, Australia, Japa

Cover: Foto ©Andreas Hilbeck / pixelio.de

Manufactured and distributed by brebook publishing software
(www.brebook.com)

Henri Dauge

A fair philosopher

THE KAATERSKILL SERIES.

A FAIR PHILOSOPHER.

BY

HENRI DAUGÉ,

AUTHOR OF "THE GEORGIANS."

NEW YORK:
GEORGE W. HARLAN & CO., PUBLISHERS,
44 WEST TWENTY-THIRD STREET.
1882.

CONTENTS.

[iii]

 CONTENTS.

CHAPTER VII.

CHAPTER VIII.

CHAPTER IX.

CHAPTER X.

CHAPTER XI.

CHAPTER XII.

A FAIR PHILOSOPHER.

CHAPTER I.

THE "STUDY CLUB."

"Never take into your confidence or admit often to your company, any man who does not know, on some important subject, more than you do. Be his rank, be his virtues, what they may, he will be a hindrance to your pursuits, and an obstruction to your greatness." W. S. LANDOR.

WHEN Mrs. Henry Fielding, soon after her coming down in June from New York to her charming country house near Fairvalley, received the earliest visit of the rector of St. Luke's, whose church she had made the fashion by leading in its choir, she said to him, after some due and conventional conversation:

"I have promised myself, Mr. Bell, the pleasure of introducing to my Fairvalley friends this summer one of the loveliest girls I know. I fell in love with her summer before last at Newport, and now she is coming here to live, and I am going to let the best of you know her. I have a picture of her which you may look at, if you like. I do not submit it to every one's inspection."

The gentleman thus addressed put on the eye-glasses with which he had been idly toying, and silent-ly followed his graceful hostess through her suite of parlors to that little room, half-library, half-boudoir, in which the lady had her own special cozy chairs, favorite books, and bits of bric-à-brac picked up during some years of foreign travel. She was a handsome and a clever woman, wife of the president. of the railroad which ran through Fairvalley, and the real and half-acknowledged leader in Fairvalley's "best society." Flattered, disliked, imitated, gossiped over, this brown-eyed, imperious, nonchalant young matron calmly held the even tenor of her way, apparently careless of everything but her own good will and pleasure. One must be her ally or be nothing to her; she was never concerned, except by her friends, it seemed; she was unconscious of slights and stings. Some years ago she had been tested by these; she was newly-married, imprudent, gay, admired; gossip did not spare her, and Mrs. Geoffrey Howard, then the head of the aristocratic circles of the town, had set her face against the new-comer. The ladies visited now; Mrs. Fielding's force of character had made her old enemy her half-conscious dependent: but did Mrs. Fielding guess how Mrs. Howard had formerly regarded her? No living soul could say.

Mrs. Fielding paused, and drew aside in order that her companion might advance.

"That is the face of my fair philosopher, as I call her," she said, in her full, well-modulated voice.

Upon a dark, richly-carven bracket in a corner of the room stood a gilded and enameled cabinet frame, whose doors, now open, disclosed a young woman's delicate and thoughtful face. The Rev. Upton Bell stepped up to it, and lifting his near-sighted gray eyes, looked earnestly through his glasses at the finely-colored picture. It was a lengthened oval, this fair face; the features were regular, the cheeks faintly flushed, the lips sweet but firm, the eyes deep-set, far apart; and a blue shade lying between the first under-lashes and the nose gave the face a look of extreme delicacy. Spirited were those deep eyes, set in their melancholy shadows: full of thought and power the soul shone through the frailer clay. A philosopher? Was she then happy? Was she at least content? Inscrutable were those mysterious eyes; calm, those faintly-smiling lips.

"It is Drosée, but she is older," said Upton Bell, turning to his hostess at last.

"So you then recognize her?" Mrs. Fielding asked. "I understood that you were once acquainted."

"If it is old Alwyn's elder daughter, I was certainly acquainted with her," he replied, with the rude directness which frequently marked the speech of a decidedly unclerical clergyman. "She was a lovely young thing when I knew her, a few years ago. I was a divinity student in New York at the time. And they are coming to Fairvalley for the summer?"

"For longer, I fancy. They are going to live in that brown cottage on Fifth street which belong to Mr. Adrian Seaford, who is married to Mr. Alwyn's sister. He gives them the rent, I suppose, and they are coming here to economize. Mr. Alwyn's life is a series of ups and downs, as we all know, and those two pretty girls have had changeful experiences."

"I knew Drosée best."

"And admired her?"

"I don't mind telling you, after this lapse of time, that I doted on her very apron-strings!" said the Rev. Upton Bell, with a short laugh. "She was not fool enough to care for me—no woman could do that—but she was kind to me with all her cruelty. I shall like to see her again, just to be sure that I'm glad to have escaped. Consider the father-in-law I should have had, to say the least of it!"

"He is a bore, of course, and a braggart, putting on airs as a genius, and doing the work of a very average writer; but he might easily be worse. He is steady, and temperate, and kind-hearted, with all his egotism —there are worse men."

"He is loud, selfish, and pig-headed to the last degree," asserted Mr. Bell, warmly. "And as to his kind heart—can you tell me the right of that story about his poor wife?"

"I would rather not speak of that," Mrs. Fielding

said, gently but coldly. "I met her during the first years of their marriage, and she seemed certainly an admirable and superior woman then. I shall never think of her except as she was then; and neither her friends nor her daughters ever name her. Let her rest."

"But I have never believed that she was to blame," began the young man, impetuously. A slight cloud crossed the lady's face.

"Do not speak to me of her, please," she said, slowly and decidedly.

Mr. Bell bowed a little, by way of apology, and passed on to another theme.

"Tell me of the little one—Josephine—the one who called herself 'Josephus Appleblossom'—how is she?"

"They call her Blossom still, sometimes, and she looks the name; she is the freshest, gayest, most bewitching young thing—barely eighteen yet, and as innocent and honest as possible. She is also one of my favorites, you see."

"And what has Drosée grown up to be?"

"She shall speak for herself. I cannot describe

what Drosée is," Mrs. Fielding said. Her fine, full voice had a sudden tremor in it; a mist had unexpectedly softened her brave brown eyes. "I owe Drosée a great kindness; I would give my ears to be all that she is,' said Mrs. Fielding, with an enthusiasm which was touching in its soft and swift uprising. "Were she my own young sister, whom I have mourned my life long, I could hardly love her more dearly!"

Mr. Bell, amazed and unwillingly moved, looked aside and half hung his head.

"You must not make me fall in love with her beforehand," he said, with an uneasy effort to say something.

"I forbid you to fall in love with her!" Mrs. Fielding ejaculated with reviving spirit. "I have already made up my mind to win her for somebody else!"

"Heaven forbid that I should be so indiscreet as to hazard a guess on the subject! Good-bye. You will be at the meeting of the choir on Saturday? If I've forgotten to welcome you back properly, excuse me. I am none the less pleased. Good day."

And the young rector of St. Luke's walked away.

At about eight o'clock on the evening of a later day in June, a tall and rather remarkable-looking young man descended the wide front steps of Fairvalley's big summer hotel. The evening was strangely chill, and its fine persistent, drizzle was enough to exasperate any but the healthiest nature; but this pedestrian, with a broad-brimmed felt hat set rather on the back of his head, and an open umbrella held carelessly across his right shoulder, walked serenely down the street, eying the darkened sky with a look of apparent satisfaction. He was possibly not thinking of the weather at all; but of what he thought it would be hard to guess. His mask was down—a serene and moveless face, with large and gentle eyes, whose power you felt but dared not explore, and dark, thoughtful, heavy brows. He walked with a free but leisurely stride down the line of pavement bordered by wet grasses, and turning a corner by a druggist's window idly crossed the street at this point; his musing eye failed to discern an unsteady old drunkard in a bottle-green coat, who here, after much hesitation and aimless pausing, had rapidly started to cross from the opposite curbstone; and suddenly the toper reeled against the gentleman. The latter but slightly felt the shock of collision, and grasping his swaying opponent with a muscular hand, steadied him on his feet.

"Heigho! my batrachian friend," he observed, with an instant and comic perception of the old man's resemblance to a frog, "you make astonishing leaps, sir. Take care of yourself, now." As he reached the opposite side of the street he glanced back to see that the old fellow was safe, and the next thing that caught his eye, as he then passed on, was a flaunting poster announcing an approaching temperance meeting. He stopped before it a moment, reflecting on the obvious argument for the cause against which he had just stumbled, and then, admonished by a few rain-drops on his face, raised his umbrella to a more perpendicular position, and strode away in the direction of Mrs. Fielding's house, apparently evolving some fine absurdity into words as he went on, while an occasional smile lit his eye, quivered in the brief flicker of a nostril and the quizzical twist of the lip, and died again.

> "So turn up thy nose at temperance frogs,
>   And gently blink thine eye—

I'll write that by and by, and present old Stark with a copy," he said, taking off his hat, and swinging it in his hand, as he went. His heavy masses of coal-black hair were shaken like the mane of a young lion in the damp night air; his high, full forehead, with its serious, half-frowning line between the eyebrows, added dignity to his fine and striking face; it was scarcely a handsome, but a peculiar and attractive-looking man who entered Mrs. Fielding's parlor five minutes later, hat and umbrella both laid aside.

"Much better late than never," Mrs. Fielding said, giving this gentleman, who was her second cousin, a gracious welcome. "I had almost given you up, and was beginning to think ill of you. Come and be introduced to a friend of mine, who will give you a cup of tea, if you are good."

He obediently followed her into her pet room adjoining this, where, for comfort and for beauty's sake, a little wood fire, which had been lit on the brass andirons of the fireplace, took the chill and dampness out of the air drifting liberally in through the swaying lace drapery of the long window. Before the shining, old-fashioned brass fender stood a graceful and slender woman's figure, clad in a white—robe, he named it to himself, for it was made with quaint and antique simplicity, and fell close and straight. Her head was beautiful and small, with close-drawn waves of dust-brown hair coiled low at the back. She held in her hand one of Mrs. Fielding's priceless little Chinese tea-cups, and was looking down at Mrs. Fielding's little terrier dog, which fawned upon her as she stood. As they advanced, she glanced up; and Wilmer, without moving a muscle of his serious, half-troubled face, said to himself that he saw the loveliest eyes under heaven. Shadowed, deep-set, and serene, they were clear, dark blue, and the rarest beauty of a beautiful, unusual face.

"Drosée, I am particularly glad to present to you my favorite cousin, Mr. Wilmer. Miss Alwyn will give you some tea, Will, she has been dispensing it to us all," said Mrs. Fielding. "Jo, excuse me," turning towards the parlor through which she had led Wilmer, "won't you come and have another cup?"

"No, thank you," a fresh voice replied cheerily. "I am planted by this piano. Come back to me and to this sonata at your pleasure."

"At once! and Wilmer—"

"Yes, if you please," Wilmer said in response to an inquiring look from Miss Alwyn, as she hesitated over sugar or cream for his tea.

"He takes very little of either, Drosée. That is right. Won't you sit down, both of you? And since you have come at last, Wilmer, where have you left your shadow, your Mephistopheles or Mentor, or whatever he may be called?"

"Madam, he is to be blamed for my tardiness, as in general for all my faults. He has not yet come from the city; I could wait for him no longer, and have left a note for him. He will doubtless be here by and by, and tell us some rare tale of a pressing emergency in the office, or of some wonderful leader or review for to-morrow evening's paper that he was working off. Don't mind him if he does."

"Hear him! He is railing at his most devoted friend," Mrs. Fielding says to Drosée; "the very cleverest of all my acquaintances, and a man without a weakness for any human being except this young man."

"And who is he, then?" Drosée asks, looking at this strangely impressive face before her, though evading the gaze of its serious eyes.

"He is one of the editors of the N. Y. —— ——," Mrs. Fielding replies, naming the leading evening paper.

"Yes, even so," Wilmer says, in that deep and pleasant voice whose subdued music is a gift of nature, making rich the poorest words it ever utters. "And he is considered by Mrs. Fielding to be a friend of mine. I find, indeed, after some months of intimate association with him, that we feel more at liberty to abuse each other than any one else is; this, and a dissimilarity of opinion on nearly every subject of thought, affording us fine opportunities for argumentation, are the bonds of our amiable relation."

"Candid youth!" Mrs. Fielding exclaims, laughing. "There, I'll say no more. I shall return to Jo and my piano, and leave you two, who are quite at home, to sup without me; we musical ones are interested in that sonata."

"And we shall be," Drosée says, while Mrs. Fielding goes. And accordingly the young man and young woman left together converse little, moving away from the tea-tray presently, and listening silently to the swell of music pouring its full tide through the air. Insensibly, at first only in the pauses, they begin to converse with each other; of what, at first, they will never remember: but each is impressing the other with the fact that they have here confronted a character new to their experience. It is in less than ten minutes that Drosée has set Mr. Wilmer forever apart from the throng of men whom she has known, and is aware that he is more and of a finer quality than even the most highly reputed of her acquaintance. She does not look unconcernedly into his face, as she is wont to look into that of any other man; but though with timid half-glances she surveys him, she has a clear idea of his personal appearance as he sits beside her, at first with head slightly bent, in attentive silence. The look of power and repose on his fine brows strikes her; the gravity of his expression; then the rare smile she is proud to have evoked; she marks the sudden ray of the eye, the doubting lift of the eyebrow, the abrupt convulsion of laughter, the swift turn of the head and the occasions when he looks full at her. This glance only at intervals, for habitually his eyes are thoughtfully averted as he considers any abstract statement, but when with this sudden movement he turns full upon her, Drosée can look no more: for his eyes are in some mysterious way dreadful to her, threatening her self-possession and her will, and she guards these jealously. She feels a vague and unexampled fear and fascination as he looks thus upon her: all tales of diablerie and witchcraft, of the evil eye and of mesmeric art dimly recur to her; she feels, as if by instinct, that if their eyes ever long and earnestly gaze into each other his will could over-master hers.

All this time she is talking with apparent ease, her companion making brief but appreciative replies and suggestions, and she is filling him with a calm and simple pleasure. She seems to him more beautiful, more graceful, more innocently gay and unconsciously wise than any woman he has ever met—and he has known many, North and South. But now it seems to him as if it were the first time that he has met a woman who thinks without pretension, who laughs without a thought of self, who pleases without consciousness or effort.

Their talk is not personal, except so far as personality is betrayed in their opinions. Wilmer listens to Drosée's expression of convictions, the reverse of his own, with a novel willingness; whatever she says is very beautiful—in her—he thinks. By and by he remarks:

"Your views seem to coincide with those of that friend of mine who was spoken of by Mrs. Fielding. I am glad that you are to meet him. I hope that I may get some better understanding of him when I hear you talk together. Personally, he is a peculiar man," he adds, pausing.

"In what way?" Drosée asks.

"He is an elderly man, and better-read than I. Politically, he is an extremist; socially, a hermit; morally, he is simply and bitterly honest. He is called a skeptic, but though he doubts much that I am accustomed to accept, he scarcely deserves that name, in my mind. Who is it says that 'the true skeptic doubts for the sake of doubting, and therefore ends, as he began, with doubt'?"

"Was it not Descartes?" Drosée asks, after a slight pause.

"It was," Wilmer answers, with one of his sudden but mildly attentive looks. "Stark quoted it to me, and I have accepted it as true. I do not, then, call him a skeptic; he is a hard, honest thinker. I hope you will take the trouble to know him, Miss Alwyn. Personally unattractive, and rather repellent in manners, he is yet a kind-hearted and superior man. He likes my cousin, Mrs. Fielding, and she is almost the only woman who attracts him even slightly. He would be a delightful member of society, if only the right woman could move him to enter it."

"I think," Drosée says, lifting her deep and beautiful eyes, "that you are describing some one I once knew. He was then the editor of a magazine; was elderly, and considered extremely crabbed, and it could not be denied was so, sometimes, as a reviewer; but in private life he was one of the most devoted of sons and brothers, and to me, whom he fancied, he was the gentlest of critics and friends. His name was Stark, too—but I have no idea where he is now, though I can never forget him. Is your friend Stark called 'Doctor,' and is his name Archibald?"

"That is the very man!" Wilmer says. "The very man! And now, perhaps—"

He pauses, for on the instant a harsh, croaking voice is heard in the adjoining room, which says,

"Mrs. Fielding, I am here to make you an explanation, and to tell Wilmer that he hasn't a memory as long as my nose."

"It is he," Wilmer says, glancing composedly at Drosée, who rises; and then calmly following her movement he stands up, and looks down on her from his altitude of six feet and one or two odd inches.

"Drosée!" Mrs. Fielding's summoning voice is heard in one musical note.

Dr. Stark starts, and looks quickly at his hostess and all about him; a young girl, with an open book in her hand, sits near the light at the piano's end, but his eye passes her indifferently by.

"Ah! Miss Dorsée, is this you in the flesh?" he exclaims, still in that hoarse voice, but with an earnest note of pleasure in it, as he meets the slim, white, advancing figure of his "auld acquaintance." The ugly, stooping, bearded man and the fair and smiling young woman clasp each other's hands cordially.

"And this is Jo, whom you know by hearsay, Dr. Stark," Drosée says, turning towards the piano. "We have wondered so often what had become of you; and here she is grown up since I saw you last."

"I am very glad to know you, Dr. Stark," ' Josephus Appleblossom' says, drawing near, and extending her frank and rosy little hand.

"Josephus, let me introduce my cousin, Mr. Wilmer Randolph Wilmer," Mrs. Fielding says, bestowing on her cousin his full name, the last one having been his since his adoption by his mother's father. Jo bows haughtily to the long name, hardly glancing at its possessor. But Wilmer, walking beside her as they all proceed to take possession of the boudoir, whence a servant has removed the tea-tray and its adjuncts—Dr. Stark declining refreshments—looks attentively at this proud young face. It is dimly like her elder sister's, but its expression is so unlike Drosée's that the difference is more noticed than the resemblance. Jo's face sparkles or clouds; it is darker, and has richer tints; Drosée's pales beside it, but only to shine with a contrasted and serener light.

"Your father, where is he, Miss Drosée?" Dr. Stark is asking.

"He is in New York to-night, as it happens," Drosée says, "but we live in Fairvalley now, since Monday."

"He is not gone abroad then, this year?"

"No; he has not been since year before last."

"Strange!   When I returned from Colorado I inquired for him, in the hope of learning how you did, and every one has told me he was in Europe.   And now you are come to live in the country.   Do you like it, Miss Jo?"

"The country? I shall make it a point to like it. It's very trying to dislike the inevitable."   She turns her sparkling face towards him as she speaks, but Wilmer catches a glimpse of a most bewitching dimple.

"Is that your best reason for enduring it, Josephus?" Mrs. Fleming asks.

"It is the wisest.   *You* are the pleasantest," Jo answers, with ready wit.   "Oh, I think I shall like Fairvalley very much.   I only wish people wouldn't let cows go on the roads; I *object* to them.   I have a weakness for cows, in a landscape, cattle grazing near a stream, and so on, but I can see nothing but terror in them unless there's a five-barred gate between us; I am then prepared to admit that they look pleasing, pastoral, innocent.   But the gleam in a cow's eye when she knows the five bars are all down!   *Exit me!*"

A burst of laughter greets Jo's plaint.

"You must have some lively recollections of such a situation, Miss Alwyn," Wilmer says to her.

"Lively doesn't express it," Jo returns. "But it taught me to respect the masculine element of society as never before. I have never hectored my cousin Louis as I used to, since," with a glance at Mrs. Fielding, whose smile implies a knowledge of the cousin referred to.

"And what have you been doing since I saw you?" Dr. Stark asks of Drosée. "Your face does not tell tales. Have you been a student or a belle these three years?"

A faint smile curves Drosée's lip, but Jo answers for her promptly.

"She has been everything, Dr. Stark! She is called a saint and a blue-stocking, a flirt and a philosopher. 'You pays your money and you takes your choice.'"

"I do not ask what she is called, but what she is," Dr. Stark replies, looking at Miss Jo rather severely.

"Oh, that she can never tell you—she is as busy finding out as others are," Jo says, but slightly abashed.

"I have been reading—I have been writing,"

2*

Drosée says, in a low, quick voice, as if bound in duty to answer her questioner. "I think in doing both I have profited. by your instructions; I have never forgotten any of your advice."

"I shall come and examine you on that point some day," Dr. Stark replies, well pleased. "Wilmer, I wish you could say as much for yourself!"

"I wish Miss Alwyn and I could compare notes on your lectures, most learned professor. I am sure you uttered fewer paradoxes and absurdities when you talked with her."

"I remember one thing you said to me, which I shall never forget," Drosée says, looking at the doctor. "Do you remember telling me that my stories had not sufficient plot and incident?"

"Yes; it was your diction and character-painting that was good."

"Thank you; but you said to me once—it was a fine illustration—'The incident of a story is what the skeleton is to a body: it justifies the movements and accounts for the form.'"

"That was a good word, professor," Wilmer says, and Mrs. Fielding nods assent.

"And you have tried to act on this suggestion?"

"I have tried earnestly."

"And with all your studying and writing, you have found time to go into society? I am surprised."

"*We* were discussing the uses of society," Drosée says, with a certain *naïvete*, turning her deep blue eyes on Wilmer, and pausing for him to reply.

"Study does not unfit one for society, surely," Wilmer says; "although with some people 'a bookish man' is considered a synonym for a recluse. Books really ought to form in one true social instincts. Similar tastes for them, forge bonds stronger than iron; and think, if the whole nation admired the same book, what a general handshaking there would be!"

"That is true!" Mrs. Fielding exclaims. "I know I always have an added respect for anybody who cares for my favorite poems—Lowell's—and how I thank any one for daring to detest Milton with me."

"My liking for you, Wilmer, first began in an exchange of remarks on the subject of De Quincey," Dr. Stark observes. "I was pleased with your admiration for a writer too little appreciated now."

Wilmer lifts his large and musing eyes, and smiles.

"Yes, I admire De Quincey: he was not a great thinker, because he did not choose the greatest subjects to think upon: but he spoke clearly; he never wrote a sentence that didn't sparkle; and his diction is more superb than Macaulay's—it is better bred, and never puts on airs."

"Capital!" Jo cries, with sudden vigor. Then she stops short, and colors royally. "I beg your pardon for that shout," she says, looking rather timidly at Wilmer, "but you just hit Macaulay so fairly! I must thank you."

"Jo was over-dosed with Macaulay last year," Drosée says, regarding her young sister with a bright and tender smile.

"Do you read with your sister?" Dr. Stark asks, turning his regard on Jo, too.

"During the last year we have read together," Jo says, gayly. "I couldn't stand it alone, when she went to reading; and so I have taken a vigorous plunge, and make for Prof. Draper and Max Müller, with all my native audacity. I rather like it now. It was a little rough at first."

"She lightened the way with nonsense," Drosée says; "when she was reading about Buddhist Pilgrims she likened the great Hionen-thsang to Baron Munchausen."

"And no wonder, with his story of the cave, and the shadow of Buddha, and such stuff," Jo retorts, scornfully. "And the way he went on! The top of a certain mountain reached '*to the sky*'—Pile it on! I said, meekly,—' and snow has been accumulating there ever since the world's beginning'—Oh, *pile* it on! I gasped—and then Drosée shut the book, and told me that, as Tuckerman said of the French, 'a frivolous temper everywhere and on all occasions signalizes them,' even so it did me!"

Jo's manner is irresistible; they are all laughing with her.

"But don't you read novels?" Mrs. Fielding asks.

"Bless me, yes! We've been reading Auerbach's through this spring and summer. Why, we're a regular literary club! We read and then we discuss, and quote and copy our favorite bits, and get up regular sermons on some texts our author furnishes. Drosée got thoroughly excited over them sometimes; but her eloquence is sadly wasted on so small an audience as I !"

" I wish we might increase it," Mrs. Fielding says. "If reading-clubs did not always come to grief—"

"It need not be a reading-club, exactly—and it need not go any further than the present company," Dr. Stark suggests, rather eagerly. "Yet I think we few friends might enjoy meeting each other at stated times, and taking up in turn some new or favorite author for joint discussion—what say you, young ladies, and you, Wilmer?"

"I think we girls could learn a great deal in such a club, and enjoy it very much, if you all would like to try it too," Drosée says in answer.

"I know that this member could enjoy nothing better," Wilmer assents, cordially.

"Don't let's have another soul!" Jo puts in. "Let's have just ourselves—don't you say so too, Mrs. Fielding—unless Mr. Fielding cares to come with you?"

"He will not be likely to care for our discussions of authors," Mrs. Fielding returns, suavely. "And—poor Henry!—his railroad business takes him away so much that I fear I need not include him in any little plans of ours. Yes, it is better to confine the membership to five, or at least to agree to admit no new member except by a unanimous vote."

"That will be pleasanter and wiser," Dr. Stark says. " Nothing is so fatal to unanimity in a good effort as the presence of one dull or unsympathetic person. But you, Mrs. Fielding, are too popular to undertake to enjoy anything quietly. You will be pestered with admiring friends who will desire to join any group you enter."

" If any one offers to join this club whom we don't want, we have each of us sufficient wit to dispose of the application, I trust," Mrs. Fielding says. " No, a larger or more thoughtless club will be profitless. Are we agreed ?"

They are agreed. And adherence to this agreement is to cost most of them some favor, and give all of them much satisfaction.

"Do you think—do you think, Dr. Stark," Drosée says, turning to him with an air of deference which marks her manners to her old instructor, "that we might find it well to arrange it so—each writing the name of some author he or she desires to study or discuss, to cast our votes together, read the names aloud, and if one is not chosen by the first votes, to try again until two or three agree on one, that one then to be given out to be studied for the coming meeting?"

"That will doubtless work well. I see that you have executive abilities. Can you think of some method of directing our disquisitions systematically?"

"Can some one suggest something?" Drosée asks, glancing around. Her eyes meet Wilmer's.

"We should like to hear you speak," he says gently. He is never over-eager to speak himself, and he is now absorbed in observing others.

"Suppose we appoint one person to give a reading from the chosen author," she says, after a trifling pause, "and another as essayist, and a third to quote any bits he or she wants discussed; and then have the meeting end in informal conversation on the author's theories, style or subjects, as they suggest themselves for dis- cussion."

"And let it end with music," Jo adds, earnestly. "Who says yes?"

"Aye, aye," Wilmer's deep voice responds, and "Amen!" Dr. Stark adds devoutly.

" Music is now in order," Mrs. Fielding observes, rising. " Drosée, come and sing for us."

" Please to consider the injustice of such a demand !" Drosée replies. You can delight us so easily, Fanny, that you need no assistance in giving us music."

" People are tired of me by this time," Fanny Fielding answers, rather uncandidly, well knowing that her fine soprano voice is the marvel and delight of all listeners. She sits down at the piano, and begins playing with careless ease.

" Find yourself some songs among my books here," she says. I will begin, but I shall not excuse you after this," and forthwith her fingers ripple into a prelude, and she is singing an air from the *Grande Duchesse*, her full, superbly-trained voice rollicking through the gay notes with the ease and careless grace of a bird's warble. With every style of music her versatile talent has made her familiar; she will sing German ballads to break your heart, and gay little French *chansons* to set you laughing ; Italian arias to melt or astonish you, and American songs of every degree, high and low ; and before you know where you are, a burst of Irish minstrelsy, or the lilt of a quaint old Scottish lay, have

2*

carried you a thousand miles away again. Her classic music is not less finely rendered for her daring Catholicity of tastes; in a word, the willful woman who would have her way, in spite of every one is wont to be admired for her independence even by those who would rule the tastes of others strictly by their own.

"Come, have you found something?" she asks, breaking off after her first song.

"I will try this," Drosée says, attempting to lift one of the heavy music books which Dr. Stark has placed before her on a table. Wilmer takes it from her, and carries it to the piano. Mrs. Fielding glances at it, and is prepared to play the accompaniment. Drosée pales a little, and stands very straight beside her friend. The song is that brief and exquisite aria of Mendelssohn's, "O rest in the Lord." Drosée's voice, scarcely so powerful or well-trained as her friends, is still an extraordinary one, a contralto of unusual range and sweetness. Her manner is excellent, and the deliberate, full notes sound forth, satisfying and pure; "wait patiently for Him and He shall give thee thy heart's desire; and He shall give thee—thy heart's desire." There is something royal in the calm from which these words distinctly come.

She sings no more. That one brief song, and that fair and gentle singer go linked in pure companionship in the minds of Wilmer and Dr. Stark, as they go, rather silently, homeward together. They are spending the summer by agreement with each other at the Fairvalley summer hotel, near Fifth street, on which fashionable street the Alwyns are to live, though not above any of the terraces or behind any of the be-fountained lawns which make beautiful that neighborhood. Theirs is the one little cottage, a brown one, set back behind some ancient elms, which ingloriously fills its narrow space. The gentlemen have been given permission to find their way thither, and their club-meeting is to take place there next week. The duties of the evening have been allotted, and the name of the author to be studied fixed upon; and so the male members of the party go, and Drosée and Jo, who are to remain at Mrs. Fielding's for the night, are upstairs preparing for sleep.

" Drosée," Jo asks, stroking her own beautiful long

brown hair with her brush. "Drosée, do you think we are going to *enjoy* that club?"

"Who can say?" Drosée answers, absently. Then she turns and kisses her sister tenderly.

"Jo, you will have a good chance to know Mr. Wilmer. Take the trouble to do so: He is superior to the run of men—wise, sensible, and rarely modest withal. You should be more gracious to him than you usually are to men."

"I will, if you make a point of it," Jo answers, returning her sister a snatchy little caress, and then hopping into bed. "I do not mean to be disagreeable to people—but, as a rule—good heavens, Drosée, how I do hate my beaux!"

And with a sigh Josephus Appleblossom turns away her face and promptly falls asleep.

CHAPTER II.

DANGEROUS GROUND.

FROM THE GERMAN.

BENEATH the sloping roof of the brown cottage
Drosée sits on this warm July afternoon, and, lazily fanning herself, scans the prospect below.   A wide-pathed,
ill-kept old garden, shaded by a few fruit trees, is in the
rear of the cottage.   In the shadiest corner, close by
the fence, a broken-spirited and humble-minded dog,
who seems to have been rented with the place to the
new-comers, lies dozing dreamily.   Next door—as Drosée can see by craning her head out of the window to
look—is the beautiful lawn and neat ornamental shrubbery about a new and pretentious dwelling; on the
other side, beyond the high fence, one can only see the
nodding heads of tall and slender locust trees waving

[37]

lightly over the green seclusion of a deep glen, in the rear of a solid stately old stone house, built in the form of an octagon, one side partly vailed in ivy. The little cottage, set far back behind its neglected, shady yard, is not at all in keeping with the showy villa, or the stately country-house. But Drosée and her sister look unenviously on the superior elegance of their neighbors; they have a calm sense of superiority to their outward lot, and have come to take their ups and downs in life with serenity.

"We have been in worse places in our time, Drosée," Jo says, cheerfully.

"And shall be again, very like," Drosée answers, with a little wry smile.

Upon a rickety rocking-chair near the bureau Josephus Appleblossom has cast the burden of her round and fair young frame. She is grimly enduring the heat, and scorns to temporize with fans. The last half of her nickname suits this girl; the tender white and soft flush of appleblossoms is in the coloring of her fresh face; her hair and eyes, her lips and brows, her eyelashes and dimples all have the glow and glint of youth in them; the early bewitching Maytime is expressed in her, but the name has been hers ever since her babyhood, when her lisping tongue twisted Josephine into Josephus, and added " Appleblossom " in compliment to the color of a new dress. Drosée sometimes shortens the long name to " Jo," and their father to " Blossom ;" but this latter title displeases her highness, who has no sentiment, and only tolerates a trace of it in Drosée, whom she admires, reproves, laughs at, and truly loves.

These are the only children of a man whom many of us have seen, dreaded and despised—John Alwyn, *littérateur*. His face and bearing attract attention, even on Broadway. He is very tall, and only a little too stout; his head is large, his forehead massive, and graced with silvery curls; his frosted beard, his gray-blue eyes and ruddy cheeks, make his face seem handsome unless it is closely studied. He has written books, few successful, and many more or less unprofitable ; he has wasted two fortunes, his wife's, and that inherited from an uncle; he has been dramatic critic, playwright, poetizer, traveling correspondent, editor ; and now, unvalued and unemployed, he still so loftily holds his head, and so boastfully recites his virtues and honors that he imposes on the unwary still, though the wise know him as sponge, braggart and bore.

His present country retirement he announces is for the sake of his health, which is suffering from too close mental application. His dismissal from that paper of which he was recently an editor, he represents as a resignation, and avers that he was killing himself, doing the work of three men of ordinary brains. Fairvalley is a charming place to recruit in, he patronizingly affirms. It has passed from an old pretty village, in the midst of a pleasant farming country, to be a town, and is latterly called a city. Farms have been cut up into building sites. Most of the owners of its showy villas are wealthy men going to and from their business in New York daily. Some very rich people, as the Fieldings,—" our friends," as John Alwyn says— have handsome country-seats here, and come to them only for a few months in the year. In summer and fall the carriages which flash along the pleasant drives of Fairvalley tell the story of the predominant wealth and ease of this flitting population. The summer boarder comes to Fairvalley, the " Fairvalley " and the " Statham " houses which have their weekly " hops," and many small boarding-houses flourish through the summer season. The little city has its newspaper, its handsome bank, and public school buildings, and the spires and towers of some six or seven churches rise here and there through the valley.

The prologue to the little drama, played upon this scene, has been spoken, perhaps; but before the curtain fairly rises, before the footlights flare up, let the friend of the two youngest women who move in the play ask you who look on to have no prejudice against them because of the bad blood which flows in their veins. No taint of their father's sordid nature is to be found in them; they both resemble that once proud and beautiful creature who was their mother, although they know her not. Her sorrow and her patience look dimly sometimes from Drosée's strange, deep eyes; her native gayety breaks out in Jo's fitful brilliancy; her proud reserve lies beneath all in the steadfast hearts of her daughters, who in their different ways have learned to rise superior to circumstance and to keep their own counsel.

Whatever other charms they have, their beauty is an evident one; and already Fairvalley is aware of that.

Jo's fair and glowing loveliness, her keen, observant brown eyes flashing the danger signal above her rosy lips ; and Drosée, with that strange youthful serenity and certain power sealed on her white brows, and shining in her deep eyes—they have already become marked amid the throng of new faces in church and promenade ; and already visitors have been admitted through the recently cobwebbed gate to call upon " Mrs. Fielding's friends at the Elm Cottage—the Misses Alwyn, you know."

Mrs. Geoffrey Howard can show no undignified haste, but her married daughter has called upon our new-comers, and expressed a dignified hope that they would attend Trinity church instead of St. Luke's—these being rival parishes, the advantages being decidedly on the side of St. Luke's since Mrs. Fielding became one of the choir. It was an undignified proceeding in the eyes of the Howards, but it had been a very effective one.

Drosée and Jo chat idly through the drowsy heat of the early afternoon ; it is cooler, and Drosée has begun to dress, when a card is brought up to her by the old and faithful servant who is their maid-of-all-work— Mr. Wilmer has called ; has asked for Miss Alwyn.

"He asked for us both, Jemima?" Miss Alwyn half asserts, half inquires.

"No'm, he didn't, neither. He asked for you both when he called yesterday and Miss Jo was gone out. He didn't ask but for you to-day ; and he's got a buggy and a little darkey waiting at the door, so maybe you're going for a drive."

"That's not likely," Drosée answers, tying a black lace scarf lightly around the neck of her simple white linen dress, and hastily plucking a crimson, summer-scented rose from a vase of flowers near. "Get up and dress, Jo. There is some mistake."

"No, there ain't," Jemima says, retiring. "You keep still, Miss Josephus."

"He has made friends with you, Drosée," Josephus says, lazily rocking. "It's very sad, but men do take to you most, I notice. Go to drive if he asks you—I shall sit up here consoling myself with the belief that if I had had him all to myself for an hour yesterday, he might have chosen me again to-day. Bless you, my children."

"It is such a pleasant afternoon for driving," Wilmer says, almost immediately after Drosée's entering the parlor, "that I have ventured to bring a buggy around, and to ask you if it would be convenient to take a turn about Fairvalley with me. If not"—as Drosée did not at once reply—"I will tell the boy to take the horses back. Don't go if you're not in the mood for it."

Drosée lifted her musing eyes to his with a far-away look, clear and rather sad, which chilled Wilmer's eagerness. He saw that she was not thinking of him. Nor was she, directly, for the moment; she was considering a former resolve of hers to let no man ever again be publicly attentive to her, or privately encouraged by her. She had determined, once for all, she thought, not to go as a young woman with young men; and her plan of the reading club had been one which meant simply intellectual contact and stimulus. She fancied Wilmer, certainly; she wanted a friend like this man, though she never wanted to have "beaux" again. But she wanted to know Wilmer at any cost! Her grave and gentle eyes fell before his.

"I should like to go," she said, hesitatingly.

"Then let us go at once," said Wilmer, joyfully. His eyes laughed; his face had changed its whole expression. He went to the door, and held it open for her to pass.

"I will be down in a minute," she said, and ran lightly upstairs.

In three minutes they were side by side in the buggy, the little darkey had disappeared, and a pair of powerful and spirited horses were whirling them down to the broad avenue.

"Have you any choice as to the direction in which we shall drive?" Wilmer asked Drosée.

"No; I have been through the city with Mrs. Fielding, and out some distance beyond her place, but I have been nowhere else as yet."

"The hills about Fairvalley are beautiful in their way, quiet, safe and placid, nothing rugged nor imposing; but the best drives are through and over them. I will take you out this way, I think."

They left the crowded avenue and whirled through a side street, crossed the railroad, and then were carried at a steady trot down a long turn of level country road.

"I want to ask you, Miss Alwyn," said Wilmer, as they rolled along, " to let me take you—and your sister, if she will—to hear a man in the town to whom I think

you will like to listen.   He always affects me curiously
—he is a clergyman "—looking at her abruptly.

"Of what type?" Drosée asked. "I know one clergyman here—Mr. Upton Bell.   I missed his call the other
day; but I knew him years ago, as a student. He is an
Episcopalian."

"I have met him," said Wilmer.   "I do not attend
any church regularly, and my family is Presbyterian,
but I go to hear this gentleman very often while I am
here.   He is a New Englander.   He is a rare man.   Of
his private life I know nothing except that he is over
fifty, and unmarried.   His face and figure are thin—
almost emaciated.   His wasted appearance and firm,
severe mouth suggest the ascetic.   But his eyes are
limpid and large, and burn with a serene flame; his
forehead is high, but broad also; his manner of speaking is composed and forcible, and he is as charitable and
liberal in his views as he is thoughtful and pious.   A
rare compound in short—a student, but also no mean
orator; for his eloquence flows as calm, as bright, and
as resistless as a mighty river.   Many admire him few
appreciate him.   I wish very much to have you hear
him."

" I can go with you almost any Sunday.   My father does not often attend church, so that Jo and I, who always go together, are free to choose our own place of worship.   We were bred Episcopalians, though, and I understand that Mr. Bell claims us as his parishioners— but then Mr. Bell is a young clergyman yet, and one can scarcely regard him with any feeling but that of good comradeship.   One's imagination cannot be useful when one knows a good, jolly, quarrelsome young fellow, through and through.   This pale and learned and peculiar preacher whom you describe, would in any case have a stronger hold over me because of my ignorance of his personal history.   I—I do not like to know people too closely—unless I can afford to lose my faith in them. It is good to reverence—any one.   And if your preacher seems great and good to me, I hope he will never pay me pastoral visits, take tea, and let me learn which he prefers—brown bread or white."

Wilmer looked down at her with attentive eyes, and a slight movement of the lip as if he would like to utter words suggested to him by this speech of hers ; but the questions that sprang up in his mind were too personal, and he put them aside for the present, saying :

"This gentleman—Dr. Bampfyle—is an Episcopalian also. His health gave way in the large city in which his parish was, and his doctor recommended rest and change of air. Rest is impossible to this style of man, but he made the change of air by coming here to preach for the rector of Trinity Church during his absence in Europe. Your friend, Mr. Bell, has St. Luke's, the new church. There was a grievous split in Trinity, and a couple of years since certain members withdrew, formed a new parish and called a new pastor. There has been much bad feeling between the two parishes. Trinity Church is an old and decidedly ramshackle edifice, while St. Luke's has been erected on a lot given by a former vestryman of the - old church, and is very new and modish indeed. The affair has many comic aspects. The squabbles of the leading ladies especially divert the curious and idle mind. From all this warring, I doubt not, you will keep aloof."

"Why do you think so?" Drosée asked.

"Pardon me—I think you reflect and philosophize too calmly to be hurried into unreasonable action," he said, with a candid and deliberate air.

"I am like other people—I reflect very profoundly —*after* acting," she replied, smiling. " Philosophy is apt to come in only to keep the peace among angry consequences." Again Wilmer looked suddenly and attentively at her; and was about to speak when she asked:

" How did this tempest arise ?"

" In a mere nothing—a question of flowers or no flowers on the altar of Trinity, I believe. A certain lady in Fairvalley began sending floral decorations for the altar during the Sundays following some holy-day four or five years since. Some people objected, the vestry was divided in its views, the rector sustained the flower party and triumphed. The choir was poor, and was recruited by several boys, who sang responsively. Another discussion, I forget which, came next, candles or a cross. Finally, the rector was presented with some kind of a purple silk vestment—I don't know the name of the thing—and he wore it on a high holy-day. It is said that he elevated the bread and wine before administering the communion, and bowed to the altar. Hideous error ! If he had murdered a baby he couldn't have been more deeply abhorred by

3

certain people. But, grant me grace, Miss Alwyn! Here I have been running on, forgetting entirely that you must have your own views on this subject, being an Episcopalian. Forgive me if I have said anything wrong. Are you High Church or Low Church?"

He stopped and looked at her with a serio-comic anxiety.

"You have said nothing wrong, Mr. Wilmer," she observed, smiling. "But you have so interested me with your recital of church difficulties that I have just discovered that this is beautiful along here. Look about you."

They had begun a long and rather rugged ascent, winding between two hills. On their left trees rose along the steep decline to meet the sky; at their right lay an old and ruined mill, and a long clear pool of water reflecting the hill-side beyond and the blue sky, with its moving fleecy clouds.

"There lies the reflected landscape," said Drosée, "'a rhyme to the eye;' what a beautiful word that was to say of the water!"

"But this hill at our left leaves us all in shadow,"

said Wilmer, after a moment's pause—"wait a few minutes."

He urged on the horses, and by and by making a sharp turn around the hill, they came out on a high level bit of road, glorious with fine lights and shadows from the evening sunshine. Far, far ahead the hills lay bluer and bluer, fainter and more faint, capped by golden clouds in shadowy domes and spires. It was like a glimpse into the far "celestial country," dreamlike, faint and golden in a sunlight fairer than that which fell on solid earth. Both of the two young people looked with a half wistful and a lingering delight upon that lovely country. Wilmer's eyes left it first, however, and with unobtrusive gaze looked upon the face beside him. There were moments when Drosée's pale loveliness had an unwonted brilliancy more striking than the richest beauty, and this was one of them. Her eyes were larger, deeper, softer and more brilliant than any Wilmer had ever seen; her exquisite features had lost both the pallor and pathos of ordinary repose, as also the bewildering variety of her animation, and so heavenly sweet was this fair face, transfigured in the rare faint sunlight, that it was no wonder that it moved Wilmer, whose grave countenance and studious ways were the native mask of quick and keen emotions which sprang responsive to the touch of all beauty and pleasure. He was only half aware of the potent charm that was already beginning to be exerted over him; but he drank deeply of a strange delight, and was called back from his reverie, and Drosée from her dreams, with a sharp shock, as the horses, weary of standing, suddenly began to move.

He gathered up the reins; as he did so, Drosée, by a sudden, soft exclamation warned him of some mischance, and glancing around, he saw that her parasol had fallen from the buggy. Bringing the horses to an abrupt stand-still he leaped lightly out, and went back for it; but as he restored it to her hand, the horses again started away. A sharp turn and a rocky declivity was before them. Wilmer had no time to regain his seat, so he seized the reins and attempted to check them as he stood. It was not so easy. He was stalwart and sinewy, with muscles of steel; but he was at a disadvantage, and the horses, one of which was disposed to be vicious at times, were excited and powerful. As he grasped the reins Wilmer looked up to Drosée. Their eyes met—both looked as quiet and self-possessed as if in a parlor.

"If you will keep your seat," he said gently—a furious jerk at the reins broke his speech.

"I will be perfectly quiet," she answered, with a voice whose composure touched him more than any tremor could. The next two minutes were a whirl of rapid hoofs, hurtling pebbles and stones, flashing tree-trunks—then there was a turn, a cruel wrench to the buggy, and Wilmer, still holding the reins with a hand of iron, left Drosée and most of the buggy upon the rocky road. He did not let go. He would check them now —they felt him at last, he thought—and then something—leather or buckle—snapped—he was flung side-long, and lay stunned against the wooded road-side, while the horses' hoofs ran resounding in rejoicing thunder down the long and sweeping hill.

When he opened his eyes again to the light of day something cool and wet lay on his forehead, and the pale and beautiful face of Drosée was bent closely and anxiously above him. Half uncertainly he lifted his hand; it was met and clasped by hers; she was all pity and gentleness, surely; a thrill went through his frame, and as he struggled to live and listen to her speaking, he lost consciousness at the first word she uttered.

When he found himself again he was lying in a softly-rolling, roomy, shabby old carriage. His head was supported softly against a woman's arm; his eyes sought her face, and then he shut them again for fear that she might move if she found him thoroughly alive! The next moment he conquered this selfish impulse, and said, in a low voice, "Miss Alwyn."

"Are you in pain, now, Mr. Wilmer?" The soft voice was anxious, but firm.

"I do not think I am. I feel heavy. Let me rise —I should not incommode you so."

"You had better be quiet, I think," Drosée said, observing how really difficult it was for him to move. "You have been placed here as comfortably as it was possible to bestow you"—and she smiled, glancing at the large and long-limbed figure reclining in such narrow space; "we are nearly home again. That is, we are near Mrs. Fielding's."

"Have I been unconscious?" he said, beginning now thoroughly to remember what had passed. "Oh, what did you do? to leave you alone so—it was abandoning you!"

The accent in which he spoke, the struggle with which he lifted his head and let it lean again upon the hard cushions rather than seem further to impose upon the companion of his misadventure, brought the ruddy and unwilling blood to Drosée's cheek.

" You managed to make me feel less indignation at your desertion than anxiety as to what country you had traveled into," she answered lightly. " I found you stunned or fainting, and tried to revive you with water from the little brook which flowed down by the road; and then, by and by, a man came by with some wood, and I got him to go to the nearest house for help, and the people very kindly sent us their carriage and two men —a driver and another—who bundled me in here and put a plank in after me, and you after that, and since you are alive again, I think we may begin to reckon up our ' many marcies,' as Jemima says."

Gayly, to cheer him, not rapidly, lest she confuse him, Drosée had given him this account of their rescue, and, as she ceased, the carriage stopped, and then moved on. They looked out. They were entering Mrs. Fielding's gates.

"You are going to stay here to-night?" he asked.

"No. But *you* are going to stay here till a doctor has seen you and said you are not seriously hurt," Drosée answered, coolly. "I decided for you while you were—away. It would be your cousin's choice."

Wilmer looked at her in silence a moment, and then a smile revisited his wan face. He bowed a little, with that whimsied look on his features.

"Thank you," he said soberly.

The carriage stopped. Mrs. Fielding, who had just dressed for the evening, was on the front piazza. Drosée leaned across Wilmer, and called to her from the window :

"Fanny! Be good to us! We have hurt ourselves."

The coachman and his companion on the box had descended, and opened the door to lift Wilmer out. Mrs. Fielding ran down the steps. To every one's surprise, Wilmer got out with a little help, and stood erect, a little giddy and bruised as to brow and shoulder, but not much hurt after all. He held out his hand to

Drosée; but on touching hers found it very cold and lifeless.

"What is the matter?" he cried, bending forward.

"She is so pale! What is wrong with her?" Fanny Fielding asked, hurriedly pressing forward at his side.

They saw now that Drosée's white dress was torn and muddy, and wet with blood; and Drosée, courage and good cheer gone, the urgent need being over, had fainted on making the effort to leave the carriage.

One of the men helped Wilmer to lift her out—helped Wilmer, who, had he been himself, could have carried her easily upon one arm; they took her into the house and into Mrs. Fielding's own room, and laid her upon the bed; and presently one of Mrs. Fielding's men galloped off for a doctor. Drosée had received a deep wound just below the knee, and the blood was stiff upon her clothing. On the bruised palms of her tender hands, and on the front of her white dress were the marks of a pilgrimage they could scarcely credit—on her hands and knees she had crawled to Wilmer, and from him to the brook for water. The men found her holding his head upon her knees, and bathing it

8*

and no one had dreamed that she was hurt until the brave lips were silenced and she fainted from exceeding pain.

"Wilmer," said Mrs. Fielding, as she sat in the parlor with him that evening for a while, after the doctor had come and gone, and Drosée had gone to sleep at last. "Wilmer," said Mrs. Fielding, not forgetting the dear and cherished wish of her heart even at this crisis, "if Drosée gets well, and you do not love her and marry her, I shall say you have a heart of stone! If anything could make a man go clean out of his head about a woman, I should think that such heroism would surely do it, even if the heroine were not that wonderful and gracious creature that Drosée is!"

"She is wonderful—and gracious," Wilmer said, slowly, and in a strange low voice.

"Do you mean to tell me you don't adore her?" Mrs. Fielding exclaimed, softly but impulsively.

"I mean that she is the most admirable woman I ever saw, and that, if she will let me, I will marry her faster than even you could desire!" he said, losing his reserve for an instant. Then he checked himself; and then looking at his cousin with a frankness new to her he said softly, "Strange! And I never felt the slightest wish to marry any other woman breathing!"

Mrs. Fielding laughed—a low, brief, musical note, then rose, and pressed her hand caressingly on her cousin's shoulder.

"I will come back presently, excuse me," she said; and left him to meditate upon his new found resolution. What he had spoken he meant, she knew; and what he had said of his previous lack of inclination towards marriage she also believed. He was the heir of a rich and old house, and much sought after as a "catch;" but he had always pursued the even tenor of his way, unobtrusive, unspoiled, apparently unaware of the traps laid for him, and caught by none. He had not always been a model young man; there were wild leaps of mischief and rare freaks of fun hidden in that curiously blended disposition; but he had the grace of reverence for God, for old age, and for women, which kept him always worthily beloved of them.

CHAPTER III.

"Whosoever will be free let him not desire or dread that which it is in the power of others either to withhold or to inflict: otherwise he is a slave."—EPICTETUS.

Owing to Drosée's illness the delayed first meeting of the "Study Club," as it came to call itself, was a very informal one, and held, not at her home, but at Mrs. Fielding's.

"How do you get on at home, Jo?" she privately inquired of her sister on that first evening of her return to the parlor and to society. The gentlemen had not yet come in, Mrs. Fielding was making her toilet, and Jo sat alone by Drosée's sofa. "I feel ashamed to lie here so cozily and comfortably, and leave you to meet the domestic discomforts as you may."

"Why, I'm sure you have had the worst of it, child," Jo said cheerily. "Would you take all human afflictions on your own shoulders, you Atlas, you! 1

[60]

think the hurt you have sustained is enough for one person."

"But I have had only the hurt," Drosée said, quite seriously. "And you have had a dozen things to endure."

"Oh, as to papa, he goes round to the Statham House so much to play whist with some intimates he has there, that he has been very little on my mind. He did not groan a groan the last time I asked him for some money, and he is really interested in the play he is writing; he has read me two acts of it—don't look so pitiful, it was much better than the last—and he expects to get it brought out in the fall—has really some encouragement."

And Josephus looked with cheerful confidence into her sister's face.

"I'm all right," she said, "only you go on getting well, and come back as soon as you can. Do you know that you have made another conquest during your sickness?"

"What do you mean?" Drosée exclaimed, with a faint, hot blush rising slowly.

"That old friend of Mrs. Fielding's—Mrs. Johns—

she is dead in love with you ! She almost told me so last time I saw her. Now, Drosée, how could you stand that amiable, prosy old soul for two minutes ? I never could, and yet you, sick as you have been, have chatted to her, and looked interested in her, and just won the poor old lady's very heart-strings. I should think it would be so fearfully inconvenient to be doted on."

· "I haven't found it so," Drosée said, laughing.

" And she thinks you have such sweet, confiding manners," Jo continued ; " me she considers a perpendicular and pokerish porcupine, I see ; but she thinks you so frank and open-hearted ! Now, Drosée, isn't that deceitful ? Because you know you don't confide in her a bit !"

" I talk to her as I talk to any one whom I like, and who wants to be indulged with a sight of my soul," Drosée said, with a slightly sarcastic ring in the sweet voice. " I tell her what it can't possibly hurt me to have repeated, and what it pleases her to hear—all innocent gossip and chatter ; no more. It is not a nice thing, Josephus, to be forced to learn caution, but I have taken some lessons, *malgré moi*. And I tell nobody everything."

"Not *me*," Jo cried, turning upon her. "Why, Drosée! I, who never tell *any one* anything, I had just as soon tell you every thought I have as fast as I think it! And to have you not tell me! you, who are of the confiding kind!"

"Josephus," Drosée said eagerly, "I tell you—I tell you things I resolve never to breathe; I trust you without stint; but I cannot say that I have told you my every thought. Even babblers have their fits of silence; and sometimes there are deep places under the shallows of the lightest glancing pools."

"Drosée," Jo answered, with great eyes, "you cannot deceive me. You *do* tell me everything. You couldn't keep it! Drosée, do I not know every man that has ever asked you to marry him?"

"Y——yes, I think so—I am sure of it," Drosée said.

"Drosée, did you keep anything from me about—about your engagement?" Jo asked, her blossom-like face shadowed a little, and her gay voice altered. "I often wonder and ponder over that. Are you—are you ever sorry for all that now?"

"No," Drosée said, after a pause. "One must endure the torment of love at one time or another. It all comes in the day's work. I am glad I have known that pain and conquered it. Now I am free!"

Jo looked at her sister, subdued, inquiring.

"The world is so much wider to-day than it was two years ago," Drosée said, with warmth. "It was all for the best. One must be lessoned by experience, and pay his heavy price, before one learns what bondage, what egotism, is in love; how free is the soul that fears and hopes for no personal and selfish loss or gain."

She had raised herself on one arm; her beautiful face was flushed; her voice eloquent. Poor, fair philosopher! so young, so confident of having attained! As she ceased speaking there entered Mrs. Fielding at one door, and Dr. Stark, followed by Wilmer, at the other.

"Now this looks extremely like an invalid!" Dr. Stark exclaimed, with a pleased, if unmelodious, croak. "How are you, my fair pretender?" He took her left hand, with unwonted gayety and gentleness in his look and air.

Drosée welcomed him gayly, and then extended the same hand to Wilmer, who bowed over it silently, but with a look into her eyes which said much. Her eye-lids fell beneath it, and even when the greetings be-tween the other members of the "Study Club" had been exchanged, she wore still that fine color in her cheeks.

"And upon what were you lecturing, Professorin?" Dr. Stark said, turning back to her. "I know you were lecturing—don't deny it! What was the theme, Miss Jo-sephus?"

"I forget," said Jo. "No, I don't—that is too im-polite. It was Drosée's favorite theme—the folly of personal desire or ambition."

"A queer theory for *you* to hold," Dr. Stark says, sitting down near them, and looking with gravity at Drosée. "You are too young to have learned quiet-ism by experience, are you not?"

"Am I a quietist?" she asks.

"Are you not? What is this doctrine—this philos-ophy of yours?"

She hesitates: her eyes are attracted by Wilmer's; he listens, as do they all. She is sure she has learned a truth; yet it is not just now easy to declare it.

"Will you tell us?" Wilmer asks.

"I think," Drosée says, making the plunge, but speaking slowly at first, "that the emptiness of success and the inevitable disappointment of desire, are sufficiently demonstrated by the general history and the private experiences of mankind. I think that it is proven that God alone is and can be sublimely good and great. No glory yet attained by man is worth attaining, so far as it gave pleasure to its owner: for who would be content with the lot of any of the great dead—who would be Napoleon, or Charlemagne, Cæsar, Solomon, Cleopatra, Elizabeth; or even Paul, or Moses, or Shakespeare, or Jeanne d' Arc? All high ambition overleaps the bounds of past success; we would be more than any of these men or women, blemished and unhappy as they stand revealed in the splendor of their lot. But—we learn limits; and, by and by, learn to be content that God is, and is alone great and good. So it seems to me natural, just, sensible, to renounce all passionate and disturbing effort, and continue only a calm, serene and reasonable activity, whose ends are not unduly exalted or desired."

"And what ends do you allow to be worthy of this calm and rational effort?" Wilmer asks gravely.

"The necessities of life; the study of the one excellent Being, and of His creation: the cultivation of wisdom and virtue. I wish it were one object of all men to have let toleration mark their attitude towards all nations and sects, and charity their dealings with individuals. I wish we all would gladly broaden the ground on which all men kneel together to worship one Creator, and all men acknowledge in unison 'There is one God:' the one God known under various names, by the Pharoahs, the Chaldees, all the nations of the East and West since the creation of man."

"Drosée! you talk like a heathen!" Mrs. Fielding exclaims, startled.

"That is the cry with which the philosophers are always greeted," Dr. Stark says, with a bitter smile. "You talk like a philosopher, child; a lover of wisdom."

Wilmer, who says nothing, is regarding Drosée with a serious and half-apprehensive air.

"I am talking too much," she says gently, with an apologetic look in her dark blue eyes. She withdraws her right hand from beneath her head, and lies back upon the sofa cushions.

"Not for us," Dr. Stark says, sturdily, regarding her, however, a little anxiously. "Are you tired so soon?"

"I have said what it may perhaps take me a year—a life-time—to explain and qualify," she says, glancing quickly at Mrs. Fielding and her cousin.

"No, indeed, Drosée," Mrs. Fielding says instantly; "I do not understand you always, dear; but I trust and believe in you without limit."

"And I would like to beg you to tell us more of what you hold to be true," Wilmer says, still earnestly regarding her. Then, with a smile which hides a slight tremor of the lip, "You have not told us whether love is a rational object of desire."

She looks up at him; their eyes meet, and seem to flash as steel and flint; she answers in a low voice, chill and quiet, unaware of how very deep an interest at least two of her listeners feel in her reply:

"I think that there is no greater illusion in all this world than that which surrounds this matter of love. Most women crave it, I believe; many men desire it; take it with the rest—to be beloved, to be envied, to be rich, to be glorious—these are the objects of the ambition of nine-tenths of those who have ambition; and each expects in the attainment of desire to be happy. On love, on political or ecclesiastic intrigue, on social or artistic effort, on money-getting—on these motives the play of life is written; and one man in his time tries many parts, and at the end of the play departs, cheated of desire to the last. Love, perhaps, is the most universal of all follies; but each such personal desire is petty, and attainment is disappointment. There is none of them worth a desire or a regret, and your only free soul is that which has broken away from the thraldom of its own wishes."

There is a chill silence. No man likes to hear a pretty woman utter such words sincerely. As Drosée slowly lifts her eyes they meet Wilmer's again, intent, powerful, almost reproachful. Mrs. Fielding's eyes are on the floor; Jo's pretty head is held sideways, with a half defiant dimple in her uppermost cheek; and Dr. Stark—no one is thinking of Dr. Stark—is looking upon the two who gaze upon each other.

"We have wandered far from our author," Mrs. Fielding says, almost immediately recovering herself, and speaking with great self-control and good humor, though privately longing to give Drosée a good shaking.

"Not so far after all," Dr. Stark says, glancing into a folded paper Drosée had previously held. "This first quotation—from Waldfried—touches one of the points discussed: '*I love to recall the passage in Plutarch's Lycurgus: The old men are singing, "We were once powerful youths;" the men sing, "But we are now strong;" and the youths sing, "But we will be stronger than you are!"'*"

"Wilmer, you were appointed reader," Mrs. Fielding says, turning to him graciously. "I hope you have selected a cheerful passage to read us! Will you begin?"

Wilmer rises in silence, takes a book from the table on which he has laid it, sits down nearer the lamp, and opens to his place.

"Auerbach is entirely new to me, as, I confess, are most of the writers of the day," he says. "But, under advice, I have read, in preparation for this meeting, his 'Villa on the Rhine,' 'On the Heights,' 'Eedel-weiss,' and a book of his shorter tales." From the latter he has made his selection, and he begins to read it.

The story is simple, but life-like. His manner is unaffected, calm and modest, as always; his effects apparently unstudied; but the reading is perfect in its way, and pleasant and moving is the sound of his rich and varying tones. There is no one present who does not enjoy listening to them.

What he says of his ignorance of most of the writers of the day is true. He is by birth and education a Southerner; adopted, after his Southern father's death, by his maternal grandfather, to whose name and comfortable estate he is sole heir. Wilmer came to New York to live after his college education had been completed in his native State. An observer will soon find that the education of the Southern student and man of letters is that of the past. Wilmer, naturally studious, is singularly well acquainted with Greek, Latin, and English classics; his own style of writing and speaking often seems to bear a quaint and not unpleasing likeness to that of the day of Pope and Addison; elegant, easy, deliberate, are his wonted words and ways; and they sit so well upon him, with his fine

Southern grace, varying at times between languor and fire, and so well accord with the idea called up by his dark eyes, long limbs, and quiet air of a gentleman, that the peculiarity is dear to his friends, who would not have him changed for the world. No one can mistake him for an unlearned man, although he is still unlearned in many authors of the day.

Wilmer having finished his reading, he is thanked warmly, and returns to his seat near the sofa.

"Drosée was to give us the quotations," Mrs. Fielding says.

"Dr. Stark will read those I have penciled out," Drosée says, and Dr. Stark, without leaving his seat, begins to do so.

"Scraps—semi-proverbial forms of wit and wisdom —these are to be the quotations, I understand," he says. "I have read you the first. Here is a suggestive one—' *When a rose is cultivated to great perfection, other thorns grow on it, but still they are thorns.*' "

"Oh, Drosée, are they all going to be like that?" Mrs. Fielding says, in soft, reproachful tones. Drosée smiles, and holds out her hand. Her friend impulsively clasps it, and continues to hold it as the doctor reads on :

" 'Hatred and contempt are not good, for they injure the soul. The art of life is to acknowledge the base as base, but not to demean one's self by passionate feeling against commonalty. You must remove hatred out of your heart, and be at peace in your mind. Hatred destroys the soul.'

" ' The King spoke of his consort, and of her peculiar frame of mind. The King and Irma spoke of the Queen for the first time. That Irma did so, and that the King not only allowed it, but really challenged it, was the germ of an incalculable catastrophe. In the first utterance of a husband regarding his wife to a third person, there lies a fatal estrangement and separation.'

" ' Honor pledges us to morality, fame still more, and power most of all.'

" 'No teaching, not even the highest, changes the mind of man. Only life, reflection, the experience of facts on one's self and others—this alone converts the mind. It is the misery of dogmatism that it wishes to teach as only life can do.'

" ' Most misery arises from the fact that people who have understanding, culture, and some talent, esteem

4

*themselves as more endowed, more highly gifted mor-
tals than others, and hence allow themselves the right
of disregarding ordinary barriers, and stepping beyond the circumscribed sphere of duty allotted to
them.'*

" ' *There are hours when I am the ideal of myself,
and there are hours too, when I am the caricature of
myself.   How shall I conceive the real being ?   What
am I ?'*

" ' *Throughout the world they boil with water.'*

" ' *I have suffered much through others——but I
still believe that there are no thoroughly bad men, but
that there are thoroughly egotistical ones, and that the
pushing of egotism beyond its true bounds is the source
of all evil.'*

" ' *I consider it a happiness for mankind—that there
is no unity of confession ; by this alone is humanity
preserved, for we must learn that there are different
forms and languages of the soul for one and the same
thing.   In the multitude of confessions there lies a se-
curity against fanaticism, as well as a confirmation that
one may be indifferent to the outward forms of religion;*

I mean that one may be an honest man in any religion, or even without an outward religion.'

"' *All the churches, ours and the Protestant, and the Jewish, and the Turkish, and as they are all called,—each has thus its voice in the song, and each sings according to his power, and all harmonize together, and up yonder in heaven it must sound beautiful; and each has only to sing as our Lord God has given him a voice: He knows how it will harmonize, and does harmonize, of course, beautifully!'* I think you have made some fine selections, Miss Drosée," says Dr. Stark, laying down the paper.

"And now, Jo, you will point these readings with your essay, and open up the line of discussion," Mrs. Fielding says, with a smiling inclination of the head towards the youngest member of the Club, who has been appointed essayist.

"I could not write an essay under the most favorable circumstances," Jo says, rising with a most becoming color on her dimpling cheeks, and walking towards the table. "I never should have understood the matters I have written a little about, if Drosée and I had

not talked of them together.   I don't claim any origin-
ality for these few remarks."

Her modesty and beauty are sweet enough to pre-
possess a more unfriendly audience in favor of her
" essay ;" and all listen attentively as Jo reads, in her
own natural and conversational tone :

" I think the quotations made by Drosée illustrate
sufficiently the moral tone and purpose of the novels
and tales of our author.   They diffuse about them an
atmosphere of toleration, fairness, sympathy with humanity and fine and delicate feeling.   Auerbach and
George Eliot are two of the greatest living novelists,
and both are apostles of charity.   Drosée says that ' it
is a question to be considered whether it works most good
in us to admire those better than ourselves, or to sym-
pathize with those who are only as good.'   Auerbach
and George Eliot both teach us rather to consider the
commonplace with loving attention than to admire
the ideal, though there are ideals they uphold.

" Of course we cannot read these books of Auerbach's without enjoying the simplicity and vigor of his
style, the absence of heat and hurry in the lives he
paints, the fresh kind of characters he draws for us.

We have never known people like Walpurga and Hausei, Irma and the Queen, or Martella, or Waldfried; but we feel their life-likeness, and pronounce them true to nature on instinct. I have had the pleasure of meeting some American relatives of Mr. Auerbach's," Jo goes on, lifting her eyes, and speaking in such an easy and conversational tone that no one can tell if this be impromptu or written, "and I am told that most of his characters are real people whom he knows, and who live about him; and that exquisite and life-like character of Waldfried's wife is like the novelist's own wife. He is twice lucky, it appears to me; he owns a treasure, and he knows that he does!"

"Brava, Jo!" Mrs. Fielding exclaims heartily.

Jo drops her eyes and goes on:

"The character of Martella was compared by one of these relatives to that of Goethe's Mignon. I don't think it a happy comparison. And if I may venture to make any comparison between these two great men, •I must say that I think Goethe often appears, morally, at a disadvantage beside Auerbach; he lacks the distinct respect for marriage, the fine appreciation of moral dignity in women, the delicacy and the *con-*

science shown in Auerbach's novels. I don't mean to deny Goethe's claim to the title of the German Shakespeare, his versatility, largeness and artistic truth, but I like the world Auerbach portrays better, and better still Auerbach's way of looking at it.

"A picture of our novelist which I have been shown by his brother shows him with large, open, kindly eyes, and benignant forehead, white hair, and a well-rounded and happy-looking face, pleasant to dwell upon. He is about sixty years old, I think. I have nothing further on my mind to say."

"The words of Josephus are ended!" Mrs. Fielding exclaims.

"Miss Jo, let me thank you," Dr. Stark says, as she returns to the little circle. "I see now that this club of ours is to be a delightful thing. If we do not all of us learn something at each meeting this is no fair promise of what is to come."

"It is the pleasantest method of study I ever tried," Wilmer adds.

"If Mrs. Fielding will only give us some music now," Jo says.

And this, Mrs. Fielding proceeds to do.

Afterwards, they cast their votes for the next author; Mrs. Fielding reads aloud from the slips of paper:

"Goethe, Kant, Prof. J. W. Draper, Max Müller Robert Browning."

They each write again. The next vote reads:

"Goethe, the Brownings, John Stuart Mill, Herbert Spencer, Prof. Draper."

"Shall we talk it over, or write?" Mrs. Fielding asks.

"Write!" say three of them.

The next, by a vote of three, decides on Prof. Draper, but it is immediately urged by certain members of the club that it will take more time than the interval between club meetings to study Prof. Draper for the first time; and so the meeting to be devoted to him is fixed for a month hence, and a final vote makes the Brownings, with whom all are at least partially acquainted, the study of the next meeting.

Of the further meetings of the Study Club, no detailed account will be found herein; this first is so specially recorded because of its influence in making its members better known to each other, and as a specimen of the workings of a private club, whose members were afterwards most severely and uncharitably arraigned by public criticism.

The cloud was no bigger than a man's hand, but it arose next day when the Rev. Upton Bell, visiting at Mrs. Fielding's, picked up four or five slips of paper carelessly left on a table, and reading aloud:

"Herbert Spencer, John Stuart Mill, Kant, Goethe, Prof. Draper," asked, "Who is interested in these men?"

"All of us!" said Jo, who sat by Drosée's couch.

"You girls are not reading these authors, I trust," he exclaimed, with a mixture of familiarity and command very displeasing to Her Highness. Jo lifted her haughty head.

"And if we are?"

"I venture to object, as your 'spiritual pastor and master,'" he answered, with a jesting tone but a serious eye.

"You are not our pastor yet," cried Jo, in a tone of cordial dislike. "It is ten to one we go to Dr. Bampfyle's church—is it not, Drosée?"

"Dr. Bampfyle's church is nearer us," Drosée answered, gently. "But we have heard only you preach as yet."

"I don't care a straw which church you attend," Mr. Bell said, sitting down near Drosée. "I hope you don't give me credit for being one of the squabblers over this division of interest? Dr. Bampfyle is an older man than I, and I dare say will suit you much better as a preacher. He is a nonentity out of the pulpit, because he gives up his whole time and study to his sermons, a thing I don't believe in doing. But go where you like—only I claim the privilege of old friendship, Miss Drosée, and I beg you not to get mixed up in this sort of thing. Give that old Stark a wide berth; he's no fit teacher for you—a musty, fusty, cross-grained, unbelieving old bachelor!"

"Dr. Stark has been my friend as long as you have, Mr. Bell," Drosée answered, still gently. "He is a very good man, and I have the sincerest respect and affection for him."

Jo had left the room, and they were alone.

"And I have the sincerest respect and—and affection for *you*, Miss Drosée," said the young man, with nervous directness. "You know how well I loved you

4*

years ago ; and I—I—don't be afraid, I won't make a fool of myself again—but I think you have only altered since then to grow lovelier—and when I saw you the first time after you came here, and heard that you had met Stark here already, I vowed to—to be your friend, if you would let me, and to warn you of the danger you were in."

"I thank you, Mr. Bell. What danger do you fear for me ?"

"Are you sure he cannot alter your beliefs ?"

"I am sure that he does not wish to. He congratulates me on being able to believe what he would desire to believe if it were possible to him."

"That is a wily opening he makes ! But besides—are you aware that he is intensely disliked here ?"

"I have never known myself to like any one less for that cause. Indeed, I have to fight an unreasonable feminine disposition to like a man better for being frowned upon. But why is he unpopular ?"

"He is cross-grained, bitter in politics, an infidel in religion, sharp and sarcastic of wit, and excites aversion in every man and woman who meets him ; and already I have heard it spoken of with wondering disapproval that you were seen taking a walk with him just a day or so before your accident."

"I had no idea that my movements were already a subject for gossip."

"They will be a subject for gossip as long as you live here. Do you not know how you are described? —'The beautiful Miss Alwyn—the talented one, you know—great friend of the Fieldings,' and so on. All this before your accident. *Now* you are the town talk, of course. Every one is on the *qui vive* for your reappearance. It is but fair to warn you—you are conspicuous! You will be Fairvalley's belle or *bête noir* within six months, accordingly as you guide your steps with discretion."

"Fairvalley is smaller than I thought."

"It is your world, while you live here. So take care."

"No, never my world. The blue heavens are above one even here."

"You seem to dislike the place."

"You—you have made me ill at ease in it, for the present. But I shall be myself again soon. Mr. Bell!"

" Miss Alwyn !"

" You will not take it amiss if I ask you one favor ? No ?—Well—do not ever repeat to me any more gossip, please.　I mean "—seeing the young clergyman flush fleeply at the insinuation which he knew himself to deserve—" I mean, it would be unreasonable to believe that people fail to say unpleasant things behind one's back—I give them credit for doing so, and I do not care, so long as I do not hear what they say.　It is the precise nature of what they say which is apt to move one to resentment—not the abstract, accepted fact of their gossip.　I wish to keep clear from worldliness, anger, and all uncharitableness.　Do not think it a friend's part to tell me what is said of me.　Now I will thank you for your kind intentions, and we will dismiss the subject forever."

He did not reply, for on the instant Mrs. Fielding entered.　He made only a formal call of a few minutes and then left.　Drosée, on her sofa cushions, fell sweetly and carelessly asleep, soon after, and vexed herself not a whit about the " cloud no bigger than a man's hand."

CHAPTER IV.

"If it be so, yet bragless let it be."—SHAKESPEARE.

"What then remains but well our power to use,
  And keep good humor still, whate'er we lose ?"—POPE.

"CAN you give me five dollars, father?" Drosée asks meditatively, gazing at the millinery in her lap—she is reconstructing a summer bonnet with no unskillful hand—and addressing Mr. Alwyn, who sits smoking his pipe on the little side piazza, in a fit of rare silence.

"Yes, I can," Mr. Alwyn says, not removing his pipe from his lips as he speaks, and running his hand, with some difficulty, into his trousers pocket, he brings up an old wallet and opens it. "Have you no money at all, Drosée?" he inquires, without passing to her the desired amount, which is beneath his fingers, together with other bank bills.

"Not ten cents," Drosée says lightly.

"Have you written nothing lately?" he asks, taking

[85]

his pipe between the fingers of his right hand again, and holding his money in the left.

"I paid Jemima up with my last accepted verses," Drosée answers in a low tone.

"Yes—yes—that was some time ago," Mr. Alwyn says, hastily. "Have you done nothing since?"

"Yes, I have written something," Drosée replies, quietly. She volunteers no information as to her ventures, though she will answer truly if questioned—her father's method of receiving her confidence being as unpleasant to her as she will ever permit herself to acknowledge anything to be. However, he is relentless to-day.

"Have you sent nothing away?"

"I sent some verses to Mr. Starr," Drosée answers, naming the editor of a well-known magazine.

"Refused?"

"Yes, sir."

"Poetry is a drug in the market, Drosée. I have told you so. I have some little experience in such matters which might serve you if you would condescend to make use of it. Your stories are good—have you tried any lately?"

"I sent a story to the ——," Drosée returns, with a nonchalant air. "The editor said it was well written, but not sufficiently dramatic. He says my verses are always good, however."

"I wish I could give you some of my dramatic instinct," Mr. Alwyn says, entirely unconscious that he writes, as a rule, the most wretched stuff a fairly educated man ever dreamed "dramatic;" "but you are not at all like me there. However, I suppose you sent him the poem, then?"

"I did," Drosée answers, with a glint of quiet amusement in her eye, "and he said it would suit a religious periodical better. He thought it was too pious. *I* thought it would just do for them—it was, to my mind, a piece of wickedness sufficiently refined to please a magazine whose taste for a dish so dressed is epicurean."

"Drosée, you have a fine mind, and all that prevents your success is your intolerable languor," Mr. Alwyn remarks severely. "You really care for nothing. You seem as happy when an unsuccessful attempt is curtly thrust back on you as when you receive a check and a compliment. You have no

enthusiasm, which is the one thing that makes me doubt your genius. And your lack of sympathy with me in the burden I carry is a defect in your womanliness. Family cares and expenses are wearing upon me, and making me an old man before my time. I am living mainly on charity; and you, in your selfishness, leave a father who craves genuine sympathy and practical kindness at your hands, to be satisfied with an amiable manner and a petty attention. The battle of life is too much for me," Mr. Alwyn concludes, puffing out an immense cloud of smoke, and wiping an invisible tear away with his wallet, he adds, "I stand or fall, lonely—lonely—to the last!"

Drosée's face has not moved a muscle during this harangue. Her father throws himself back in his chair, pressing his hand to his brow as if a "maddened brain"—a favorite expression with him—were even now beating there. His ruddy cheek and ponderous frame seem to indicate so sturdy a physical condition that this drooping condition appears inexpressibly droll in one of its aspects. But in Drosée's face neither contempt nor pity may gleam or glint in eye or on lip. She sometimes, as now, experiences a strong internal.

revolt against well-known pretense and tricks of manner; and, at this moment, even for the sake of peace, she cannot answer him with the soft and politic blandishments which may appease a petty tyrant. Her calm silence chills the egotist. He misses the gentleness of speech which sometimes rewards his pathetic plaints. He pulls away at his pipe again, and drops his hand from his head.

"You must consider, Drosée," he says, coldly, "that I am unable to maintain you in idle vagaries. You had better save your money for hairpins than waste it on stamps for sending ill-considered articles. My brain has been coined for money to support you two girls in idleness. When, weary and broken, I ask you to help yourself a little, you smile and say, 'I can't.'"

"Father," Drosée replies, rapidly and decidedly, "both of your daughters, thanks to the education our Uncle Seaford gave us, are able as they are willing to support themselves. We have desired to do this; but you have insisted on the semblance of leisurely ease for your family, and Uncle Seaford has added generous arguments. Meanwhile I write with the best directed

efforts toward success that I can plan. But I am not
so foolish as to expect fortune to come at the first beck.
I shall succeed," she adds, gravely, lifting the strong,
serene face. " 'Everything comes to him who waits;'
and I have one element of power in me—I am patient.
If I seem never despondent, I do not think to prove
myself a sensitive genius by fits of melancholy and
despair. I prefer to bear my small woes in silence,
and to laugh, for the sake of family comfort, which is
surely as dear to me as you could desire."

Neither Drosée nor Mr. Alwyn feel, as she speaks,
that she is sharply contrasting her mental tone with
his. Jo would perceive it instantly, if she were present; but Jo is in the kitchen making her father's
favorite pudding for dinner. Drosée's swift and
pointed summary of their real situation has its effect,
however. Mr. Alwyn rises.

"You justify yourself, as is your wont," he says,
in a voice between bluster and tears. "I trust, Drosée,
that when it is all too late you may never reproach
yourself."

He enters the house with heavy tread. Drosée sits
still and finishes putting the bonnet together with an

untroubled air. Success is on its way to her now, little as she counts upon it; her last venture on the seas, left without a troubled thought to the care of wind and currents, is successful; Drosée's ship is coming in, and she sits, unwitting, curving the stem of a rose.

"Done?" Jo says, at her side.

"Just," Drosée answers, snipping off a thread, and lifting the cream colored trifle in her hands she places it daintily on Jo's head, and falls back to admire the effect. Jo's face is a little over-flushed from the heat of the stove; but she looks bewitching in that re-modeled bonnet, and Drosée expresses her satisfaction, Jo prances—no other word will express it—into the hall, to view herself in a looking-glass, and Drosée gathering up her working materials, is about to follow, when she hears a step on the front piazza, and rising, meets her only cousin, Louis Seaford.

"Embrace me, Drosée!" cries the young man, laughingly. "I came to bring you the news from New York. Your book is to be brought out, and the publishers have come down handsomely."

Drosée's blue eyes fill with sudden radiance; then

with an otherwise serene, unstartled appearance, she takes her cousin's hand, lifts her delicate face, and receives from him a brotherly salute.

"It is very kind of you to come yourself, Louis," she says, with friendly warmth.

"Oh, very kind!" he replies, mockingly. "I always was too good natured; I can't help feeling anxious to make any little sacrifice to please you girls. Jo is alive?"

Sans bonnet, Jo comes to greet him just now, and opens her lips to say:

"Will you be good enough to talk *quick?*" In the midst of which query she is unceremoniously kissed. She draws back; but her eyes dance, her color deepens, and she looks twice as much excited as Drosée, entirely saving her the trouble of asking questions. Louis answers in his own way, but his answers are so gratifying, the facts so promising, that Jo announces that she considers Drosée's future eminence assured; and laughs and chats away in a rapture, which would be laughable if it were not so unselfish and so sweet; finally dancing off the piazza and round to the back door to tell the faithful Jemima, and to see about bringing the dinner to the table.

No one thinks of Mr. Alwyn just now!

When Jo had gone, Louis asked carelessly:

"I think one of you girls has a birthday to-morrow. Which is it, Drosée?"

"It is Jo's; my birthday is past long ago."

"Then it must be nearly here again! At any rate, I had an idea it was one of you, maybe both; *I* don't wish to be partial," jesting to cover some nervousness. "I've brought you a birthday present apiece, my dear, and will you please give hers to Josephus Appleblossom?"

"But you must stay all night, Louis!"

"Yes, if you'll let me; but do you give the things to Jo, please."

The "things" turned out to be gloves of various dainty shades and numerous buttons; and as Drosée unhesitatingly rejoiced in her share, and herself handed Jo's to her, my Lady Appleblossom, who sometimes refused the presents Louis was prone to offer her, thanked him graciously, and took the gloves.

"Mrs. Johns' little pug nearly chewed up one of

my very last pair," she said, frankly, the next morning, displaying the mangled remains, which she pulled out of a drawer in a parlor table. "Look, Louis!"

Louis looked—at the dimple in her cheek, apparently.

"You're a perfect raven in the wilderness," Jo pursued, thawing entirely.

"Your compliments have a flavor to which I am all unused," said Louis, laughing. "Try me with another, do, Josephus!"

Then he hunted about for his hat, and surreptitiously possessed himself of the mangled glove, kissed Drosée's cheek, and Jo's hand, and went back to the city and his desk in his father's office.

*   *   *   *   *

The news that Miss Alwyn had a novel in press went about Fairvalley in a very brief space of time. Mr. Alwyn was not the slowest to announce it. He was noisily proud of Drosée, and oppressively affectionate both in public and in private. He went up to spend an evening at the Statham House to play whist with other lovers of the game; and obtrusively informed his acquaintance how his care and tact had developed his daughter's "genius." Statements of his came back to Drosée sooner or later. Probably they tried her soul; but she had learned much self-control; she showed no heat, no confusion, no distress.

Dr. Stark and Wilmer both congratulated her on the prospects of her book, and prophesied kindly concerning it. She received such remarks with a manner which led Wilmer to quote to Dr. Stark the well-worn line of Pope's:

"Graceful ease, and sweetness void of pride,"

and then to frown slightly, when Dr. Stark completed the couplet, as they walked alone towards their hotel. Her modesty and candor at this time, when she was receiving a premature applause from her acquaintance, strikes her friend, Mrs. Fielding, with a fresh admiration for her.

"From her manner you would never think of her as an aspiring blue-stocking, or anything at all remarkable," she says to Wilmer. "She seems just like any other girl, does she not?"

"She seems unlike any other woman I have ever known," Wilmer replies, with gravity.—"Pardon me;

I know what you mean. She is not at all pretentious."

"Not uplifted—superior—formidable in any way," Fanny amends.

Wilmer answers by a doubting lift of the eyebrow.

"What do you mean?" Mrs. Fielding insists.

"She is extremely formidable—to me," he says. His look puzzles his cousin; but he gives her a chance for no more questions, and habitually evades all discussion of the "fair philosopher."

But not every one speaks so highly of Miss Alwyn's approachability as her friend indicates. Mrs. Geoffrey Howard, the great lady of Trinity Church, and her married daughter, Mrs. Estwick, who sings in its choir lately, and superintends her husband's superintendence of the Sunday-school, accept the Misses Alwyn as members of their church now, for they go regularly to hear Dr. Dampfyle, whose cogent reasoning, philosophical tendencies, and pure moral teaching more than satisfy them as listeners; and these two ladies call upon Drosée and Jo, and desire their assistance in teaching classes.

"Have you ever taught in Sunday-school, Miss Alwyn?" Mrs. Howard has asked. Mrs. Howard is still beautiful at fifty-five; her complexion is fresh and delicate, her snow-white hair is exquisitely arranged, and her severe but perfect profile is like that of some delicate cameo. She turns her fair face full on Drosée, who notes the beauty and the flash of the diamonds in the fine, small ear-tips with a ready admiration of so much cold splendor.

"Yes, I once taught a class," Drosée replies. "I was younger than I am now, and thought that I knew much more. I cannot venture to teach now; I am too busy learning."

"You would have only the plainest kind of work in our school," Mrs. Estwick says, quickly; she is voluble, ready, and of coarser clay than her beautiful mother. "The catechism and lesson-books are all printed, ready to your hand; surely there is no need of much talent or scope for individuality in this," she adds, with a kind of prompt spitefulness too familiar to this young matron's lip.

"I do not mind taking a class," Jo says, abruptly.

"I rather like it. I am used to it. Can you give me some to begin on next Sunday?"

"Yes, indeed," Mrs. Estwick answers, diverted from Drosée an instant by Jo's gallant sally, but returning to the charge at once. "Cannot *you* agree to teach catechism, Miss Alwyn?"

"I cannot teach at all, Mrs. Estwick," Drosée says, with decision. And then—"for our sins," as Jo says, the door opens, and Mr. Alwyn enters. The ladies are not particularly overjoyed at his advent, for he is an egotist so abandoned as to acknowledge feminine charms but slightly, and Mrs. Howard's sensitive nose scents strong tobacco from afar. But they are forced to listen to his flow of conversation for a time. He lifts his eyebrows loftily on learning of Jo's promise.

"I leave my daughters quite free in these matters —quite free," he observes, patronizingly. "I never go to church myself. I can't without criticizing ; my critical faculties are natural to me, and practiced by a long literary career. I never hear a sermon that doesn't offend me ; I always want to re-write it and touch it with a little novelty and common sense. And Drosée resembles me. Stark says—you have heard of Dr. Stark?—that she has a strikingly analytical mind. He thinks great things of my daughter."

"Dr. Stark is an atheist, I believe," Mrs. Howard says, slowly. "One must admire his abilities, but it is with a shudder I think of his responsibilities. I hope Miss Alwyn is not under his influence."

"Dr. Stark is not an atheist," Miss Alwyn says, calmly, "and I am proud to consider him my friend. I wish I could have obliged you, Mrs. Estwick," as the ladies rise; "I would be glad to prove my affection for the church in which I have been bred, by serving it in any way—but not all of us have the gift of teaching."

"Ask her to sing in your choir," Mrs. Fielding says, when Mrs. Estwick narrates this conversation to Drosée's friend, not for the first time in their round of visits on that day. "She will be a great acquisition to you in that way. Isn't Jo Alwyn a lovely girl? Mr. Alwyn—now, I beg Mrs. Estwick, that you won't think anything he says worth remembering. He is a man who has attained a certain position, of course," Fanny throws in, with a vague touch of grandeur, "but then, people of that ilk are always uttering unconsidered trifles. Drosée will sing in your choir, if you ask her, no doubt. I only wish she could be in ours. But Trinity is so near her, and of course I understand her choice."

"But is it true that Dr. Stark and these young ladies, and one or two more, have formed a secret society, and refuse admission to all applicants?" Mrs. Howard asks. "I have heard that every member of the society is a skeptic, and that they discuss German metaphysics and modern infidelity *con amore* amongst them."

"I beg to say that *I* am a member of that club," Mrs. Fielding says, with great dignity. "I am a church woman in good standing, I hope. The club is confined to a few members of studious tastes, and discusses everything in a liberal spirit. I have some curiosity to know who so distorted an account of it."

But this she did not learn.

The summer went on, July and August of it being intolerably hot. It was the Centennial summer, and excursions went over to Philadelphia from Fair-valley often. Otherwise the little town remained un-usually quiet, and Mrs. Fielding gave none of her usual garden parties during the season. She was enjoying the rare luxury of the society of a congenial few, and attempting the rôle of a match-maker for her favorite Drosée. And her club and her companions became obnoxious to Fairvalley society, ignored and left out.

Much of the idle talk that floated about was due to Mr. Bell, an inveterate gossip, and unconsciously irritated against the young women, who had begun to be noticeable members of the rival parish—for Drosée had really begun to sing in the choir when Jo took up her labors in Sunday-school—he allowed himself to make ill-natured and petty criticisms and remarks upon them. He perhaps never realized how much he was to blame for the rise of the gossip against which he had himself warned the woman whom he believed he loved.

Our fair philosopher was walking with unswerving feet a narrow ledge between popularity and hatred, admiration and envy, praise and calumny. And what philosophy will be a perfect defensive armor for a fair and young woman against all the darts of vanity or of scorn?

One afternoon in July Drosée Alwyn sat by an open window, her elbow on the sill, her forehead on her hand, and a book open on her knee. She was reading intently, and unconsciously twisting on a finger of the hand which held open her book a skein of fine crimson worsted which she had picked up in her room when she brought from it the book which now absorbed her. It was Prof. Draper's "History of the Conflict between Religion and Science," and this Drosée was reading more earnestly, more unweariedly, than most women a new novel. As she read, every now and then pausing to reflect over and re-read passages which stirred her, she sometimes broke off a bit of the gay worsted, and laid it between the leaves of her book. A fine, ragged edge of these impromptu marks showed her progress through the work. It was one of Drosée's methods of study; she had as many methods as moods. Her mind was very quick and active, and study was to her delight and not weariness. She readily grasped the meaning of her author, and followed fast and far the reasoning or the facts before her; but she always re-read and collated in her own fashion the most striking passages of works she so rapidly and fearlessly read; thus grasping a clear, assured and general idea of what she had been over. Her fine memory was often remarked upon; and it was due to this careful, self-taught attention to leading ideas and passages in works like the one before her. The pleasure of understanding gave her the delight that exercise gives to power; in hard thinking, her vigorous and growing mind strengthened joyously, as on its natural aliment, just as her gracious heart was fed by opportunity to give pleasure.

Jemima's heavy step in the hall was quite unheard; but Jemima put her head in at the door and called her.

"There's an old lady come for you in a kerridge," Jemima observed, and went back to her kitchen.

"Thank you," Drosée said, and glancing out of the window, put her whole skein of worsted in her book, laid her book upon the table, and ran lightly down the two or three piazza steps and out to the gate, all intensity, all meditation, vanished from her brow and eyes, and an alert and gracious readiness in her look and air.

To her surprise, Mr. Alwyn was before her, and stood bareheaded by the carriage step, talking to the ladies within. She had not known of his acquaintance with Mrs. Johns; but then she immediately reflected that the good lady boarded at the Statham House, whither Mr.

Alwyn frequently repaired to play whist, and doubtless he had there met her.

Mrs. Johns, a stout, motherly-looking old lady, rather too tightly encased in her rich brown silk to look entirely at ease, beamed benevolently through her gold-rimmed glasses on Drosée as she advanced; her full, smooth face, with its rabbit-nose and mouth, was as opulent in kindness as her poppy-wreathed bonnet in color.

"Come, my dear, and take a little drive with Miss Ball and me, this nice cool evening. Here is my friend, Miss Ball"—the other lady bowed—"come right along in, and bring your sister, if she would like."

This was the "prosy old soul" of whom Jo declared Drosée had made a conquest during her illness. She never would be on formal terms with any one she fancied at all, and calling at Mrs. Fielding's for the first time in her life, to return a visit she owed to Mr. Fielding's acquaintance with her husband, she had chanced to see the convalescent, and from that time had been assiduous in her attentions to her. In spite of her simple ways and occasionally peculiar grammar, she was a true gentlewoman, and Drosée, like a wand of witch-hazel detected the pure fountain hid from view, divined the goodness in the heart of this *parvenue*, and dared to enjoy her favor. She accepted the invitation to drive for herself, but Jo was spending the day with the Seafords at the Exposition.

"If *you* would go now, Mr. Alwyn," Mrs. Johns said, as Drosée went back to the house for hat and gloves, and Mr. Alwyn, for some reason, accepted the invitation with much readiness. When Drosée came back she found a seat ready for her beside Mrs. Johns, and opposite, with their backs to the horses, sat Miss Ball and her father. The coachman gathered up his reins, and Mrs. Johns beamingly bore away her friends.

"There's grander scenery, of course, and all that," the good lady observed, gently settling herself in her easy carriage, "but there ain't any country I know that looks as bright and thrifty as it does around here. We're going to take the old Bridge road towards Brakesburg, and I want you to see how pretty and orderly and nice all these little farms about are kept, Miss Drozy. I was brought up not far from here, and I like to come back to the neighborhood in summer time and drive all round the country. You wouldn't know

5*

our old place; the farm's all cut up, and the new road runs right through the old pasture; the house they've pulled down, it was getting old in father's time. I love it out here, anyhow. Somehow no air seems so sweet; and if Mr. Johns thinks he can get along, I mean to stay till every leaf is red before I go back to the city. October's the prime o' the year; *you'll* be here for that, and I'm real glad of it."

As she prattled away thus confidingly, there was an apparently agreeable conversation going on between the two opposite. Mr. Alwyn was evidently purposed to "roar softly," but still he was impressed with the idea that he was to play lion, and his companion listened with a flattering appearance of taking him at his own estimate.

Drosée noted the appearance of this fourth member of the party without being much impressed. Miss Ball looked about thirty years old, though really older; she had a handsome, rather Irish face, rich color, curly black hair, short nose, and well-cut mouth and chin. She was dressed in well fitting black, and had a red rose with many leaves in her bonnet of black straw and lace. She had the misfortune of blushing incessautly, in a juvenile and embarrassed manner, whenever pleased or interested; and yet, though her face lacked a certain look of refinement that marks a well-bred woman, it was not unattractive, being good-humored and honest. She was known to Mr. Alwyn as a distant relative of Mrs. Johns; with a very small independent income, and occupying the position of "companion" to her wealthy cousin. She had read all of Mr. Alwyn's books—one before she met him and every other one since—and felt a kind of awed delight in the notice of "an author."

The party was driving by a broad stone fence beyond which they caught a glimpse of a more neglected place than any other which they had passed, an old-fashioned farm-house just glimmering through the trees, when Mr. Alwyn suddenly addressed his daughter.

"Drosée, that was the old homestead of your mother's family."

A flash of the most vivid expression of surprise that had passed over Drosée's face in many a long day revealed itself to those who looked at her. She colored, and her eyes expressed displeasure for an instant.

Her father, with all his garrulity, had not named her mother in Drosée's presence for years. Why should he so noticeably have named her in the presence of strangers?

But the flash went as it came, and a softer look shone in Drosée's eyes as, without reply, she looked earnestly at the old house they were passing.

"You knew that your mother was born near here?" Mr. Alwyn asked, with a persistent following up of his first move.

Drosée did not look at him, but at the passing trees. Her face said absolutely nothing. Her lips said:

"I knew that she was a native of this county."

"Was your mother Emily Windham?" inquired Mrs. Johns, laying her hand on Drosée's arm. "Well, I never! Why, I never *did* hear who Miss Em married! Was it you?" to Mr. Alwyn.

"She was my wife," Mr. Alwyn said, with an air indicative of mingled pride and grief.

Mrs. Johns lowered her voice.

"And is she dead, then? She was younger than me! And such a beautiful creature! Oh, it is *her* eyes you have got, my dear!" suddenly caressing Drosée's small, cold hand. "Not the color, but the look. I wish you would tell me a little."

But Drosée's gentian-blue eyes looked with a piteous sorrow into her questioner's.

" I cannot bear to speak of my dear mother, Mrs. Johns. I—I want her yet!" And then she turned away a little.

Mr. Alwyn flushed to the deepest red, but Mrs. Johns, still pressing Drosée's hand, changed the conversation hastily by asking :

" What kind of trees are the best for shade, Mr. Alwyn?" And as he had an opinion on every subject, his reply was prompt, and long-winded.

Before the subject of trees was exhausted—for Mrs. Johns had some remarks to make about the "ellums" in the yard of her old home, and on other trees in particular, Miss Ball suddenly called to the coachman to stop, and beaming with excited blushes, explained that they had passed a bed of the very ferns she wanted, growing in that wet spot.

" Mayn't I go get some?" she asked of Mrs. Johns; and, of course, receiving consent, Miss Ball opened the carriage door and was about to hastily descend, when

Mr. Alwyn stepped past her and out into the road, and then, bowing, offered his hand to help her to alight.

As he did so, with a manner more graceful and courtly than any his daughter had seen him wear, and as the sunlight smote his dark, but silver-threaded curls and handsome ruddy cheek, it glanced through Drosée's mind that after all her father must have been once—was still, some people said—an eminently handsome man; and the reason of her mother's early love for him, formerly undiscerned by her, flashed across her. He was basely selfish, he was unreliable, vain, a thorough egotist; but he had possessed a handsome presence and attractive manners in his youth, very like. Ah, well!

Mr. Alwyn had accompanied Miss Ball back to the bed of ferns. The horses stood quietly, and Mrs. Johns waited placidly for their return. She talked on to Drosée of indifferent matters in a friendly tone. Drosée at last rose a little in the carriage and looked to see if the absentees were returning. Mr. Alwyn was giving his companion a little bunch of small ferns. Their hands were meeting—were lingering—were apparently clasped together, and they looked at each other. Drosée started—had she spoken aloud, or only thought the exclamation, "*But my mother is not dead!*" She looked with startled eyes at her companion.

"Did I—did you—speak?"

"What's the matter? I said the cows did it—ain't they coming?" referring not to the cows, but the couple in the road.

Yes, they were coming now, rather rapidly, and walking apart from each other. Miss Ball had a vivid color—but of course it was from the exertion—and Drosée was as self-possessed as ever, and talked as smoothly, while inwardly rejoicing that she had not thought aloud just now. Her mother was dead to all the world but that which knew her truly. Drosée reflected, and asked a question.

"Do you play whist, Mrs. Johns?" she inquired, before she left that good lady.

"Not often, dear—sometimes, to make up the game for Mr. Johns. *He* plays. And Miss Ball—she plays very well, too."

Drosée bowed with gentle and not unkindly gravity to Miss Ball, when the carriage stopped at the gate of the cottage.   But she did not shake hands with her, though submissively receiving the kiss Mrs. Johns bestowed on her.

Mr. Alwyn rode on with the ladies to the Statham House.

CHAPTER V.

" ' But O Thelymnia! our lives are truly at an end when we are beloved no longer. Existence may be continued, or rather may be renewed, yet the agonies of death and chilliness of the grave have been passed through; nor are there Elysian fields, nor the sports that delighted us in former times awaiting us; nor pleasant converse, nor walks with linked hands . . . nor looks that shake us to reassure us afterwards, nor that bland inquietude, as gently tremulous as the expansion of buds into blossoms, which hurries us from repose to action and from action to repose.' ' O! I have been very near loving !' cried Thelymnia. ' Where in the world can a philosopher have earned all this about it ?' "—W. S. LANDOR.

THE story of the next few weeks is best written by Drosée's pen.

"20th July.

" In this book, which is less the journal of my individual emotions and actions than a picture-book for me of persons and places which successively impress me, I ought to make some pen-and-ink sketches of the people I met a few days ago at Mrs. Howard's evening

[113]

party. It was a gathering in honor of Miss Sands, a
niece of Mrs. Howard's, who is visiting her. Miss
Sands herself is blonde, fluent and superior, is very
rich, and very well educated; names all the foreign
cities she has visited with the foreign names. Dr.
Stark accuses her of *Firenze*, but I did not hear that.
In fact, I did not see very much of her: I left those
two discussing the 'Hegelian philosophy,' and went
away with a Mr. Keene. There were a great many
men there, but nobody worth specially sketching,
though I talked with a great majority of them, it seems
to me. There was a Mrs. Lawrence I was thrown with
for awhile—a wiry, sallow, tall, short-haired lady, a
visitor here, who has a nimble tongue and a quick wit,
and paints wild-flowers exquisitely, I am told. There
was a Mrs. Gage, who dresses magnificently, and is rude
till you wonder at a person so constituted ; but even to
wonder is to pay too much attention to the disagreeable.
I met Mrs. Estwick's husband—an absurd phrase !—
but he simply impressed me as such, being much older
than she, tall, portly, and gallant, and evidently much
admired by her; her eyes followed his every movement, and she ceased her conversation when we came

near her in promenading, and finally, when I had
worsted him in some trifling argument, she, who had
just joined us, answered some slight raillery which he
received very graciously with an appearance of resentment and annoyance! Dr. Stark took me away then,
and talked about Miss Sands until I was vexed at him,
and at myself for listening.

"The chief thing I want to write down is a scrap of
conversation with Mr. Wilmer that night—alas! if I
could but catch his inimitable manner of saying things!

"We were in that lovely little glen—which I see I
have not described! Well, it is in the rear of that
large and stately house of the Howards that there is a
glen whose artificial nature is disguised by time; tall
and slender young trees have grown up upon the side
of the small ravine, a view of which is commanded by
a rustic arbor at the starting-point of the paths which
lead down its terraced descents. In the depths of this
glen lies a little lake, long and narrow, spanned by a
rustic bridge with seats on either side; and in the
lake's farther end a fountain springs in a slender wind-
tossed jet, whose spray wets the light leaves of the
young and whispering trees. The spot is so beautiful

as to quite justify the owner's pride in it. On the night of this party a row of Chinese lanterns lit its darkest recess, but where we sat, on the bridge, we saw the moon, rising, send her yellow splendor through the trees, quivering on limb and leaf. I remember drawing my white shawl about me, as we sat there, and Mr. Wilmer's asking if I was cold; to which I replied no, quite comfortable; adding that I thought only the rheumatic were excusable for preferring the parlors to the glen; when he observed:

" 'I once had a fearful experience with the rheumatism.'

" ' You ?' I asked, hardly ready to believe my ears if Mr. Wilmer was about to become that hateful thing, a man who narrates his physical distresses.

" 'Yes; with a room-mate at college.'

" I knew he was going to say something amusing, in his solemn manner. 'And this room-mate ?'

" 'Well, he suffered from it acutely every night for about two weeks,' Mr. Wilmer said, in that fine, deliberate, dreamy tone, always apparently unaware of making any comic turns. 'It didn't seem to bother him much in the day-time, you know, he could swear

at the servant boy, then, or indulge in any like friendly passages with any wandering comrade—for he was
very profane—and this seemed to lighten his mind and
cheer him. I used to wonder at the pleasant effect
it had on him. But let midnight come, and with it a
search after rest from the toils of Alcestis or Calculus,
and then, amid the quiet darkness, upon the verge of
grateful slumber, back would I be recalled by the most
piteous and unearthly yells! For the first two or three
nights I used to rise, and mix him up a dose of turpen-
tine, and camphor, and borax, and mildly urge him to
swallow it; I used to tell him it would certainly do
one of us good, you know; but the suggestion always
appeared too grim to him, and I believed that he preferred to howl anyway, for he wouldn't take it!'

"I was convulsed with laughter, but he went on,
musingly :

" 'After that I used to lie awake and listen to him
whoop—because it was interesting to listen ; nothing
could have been more so, though some things might
have been more agreeable—and I used to marvel at
the capabilities of his lungs, and wonder if they were
always so powerful, and if his parents were yet alive,

or had died when he was an infant; and *if* so, whether he was too young at the time to remember if they forgave him on their death-beds, but said they were willing to die—perfectly willing! Yes, I used to ponder over these things, and occasionally I'd howl a little myself to keep him company, or heave a chair over in his direction to divert his mind and let him know I was thinking about him.'

"24th July.

"Dr. Stark was here alone this afternoon. He surprised me by telling me that Mrs. Estwick, who is an unamiable woman, was my special enemy. I do not know how I can have offended her, unless it is that I sing most of the solos in the choir, and the organist prefers my voice rather too frankly. Her husband joined me on the street, day before yesterday, walking home from the depot, and *he* talked to me with apparent cordiality. Dr. Stark could not or would not explain. However, I should not deeply consider such trifles, and never ought to record personal annoyances. I should not have thought of it twice had any other friend warned me; but shall obey him in being careful in all my intercourse with her.

"25th July.

"Fanny Fielding is a warm-hearted, impulsive woman. It is two years now that we have been friends. I have studied, loved, pitied her. I believe few people knew her at all. Her husband's intemperate habits are known to very few, and her struggles to rescue him to fewer. This task is all the harder for her because she married him without duly loving him. She treated him very coldly when they were first married—he loved her then, devotedly. But of late years she has tried to win him back, and bears everything beautifully. With those bonny brave brown eyes of hers, she looks the world in the face boldly, serene, smiling, and apparently without a care. Her husband is a man of influence and wealth; and as he walks up the church aisle on Sundays, tall, with bent gray head and reverent air, he looks the dignified and decorous gentleman. He passes the plate with an inimitable grace, and people drop in their small contributions shamefacedly, feeling that he who holds the plate could double the sum total of all their alms without ever feeling it. I went to church with Fanny last Sunday, and sang a duet with her during the offertory.

Mr. Bell came up to us as we were getting into the carriage, and graciously said that it was beautiful, and that he wished I would join his choir! Trinity Church is closed for the present, and undergoing some slight repairs—as few as possible, for they will build again next spring.

"Fanny told me to-day, with a mixture of candor and reserve which is one of her most *piquante* charms, of her condition and her hope of good through it. In the second year of her marriage she became a mother, and her husband was passionately attached to the child, who died. 'Henry is devoted to children—notices every baby we pass on the street,' she said. 'He will be another man when he has one of his own to care for,' she added, softly. I hope he will! He is at least more attentive to her of late; and she may redeem the old error in the day of new joy and pain. Heaven help her!

"27th July.

"Mr. Wilmer is wonderful to me. I admire his ways of saying things. The other day he said, dryly, after some mocking speech of Jo's—she was chaffing Louis—'What an exquisite blending of fact and fiction a woman is! In her extremes are met—and,' with a quizzical smile, 'by her men are driven *in extremis!*'

"He and Dr. Stark, last night, were talking of the wide harm done by evil-speaking. Dr. Stark is sometimes satirical, but I never saw a man detest gossip more. Mr. Wilmer said carelessly:

"'A man may very well afford to let others make remarks about him, but he cannot afford to make remarks about himself. It were better to have two men speak ill of me than to speak well of myself once.'

"There is a rare clearness and serenity of judgment displayed in many of his chance sayings. I had rather have this man, young as he is, to be my friend, than any I ever knew, old or young.

"August 1st.

"If he is as wise as he seems to me to be, how can any one help marveling at this friend of mine? I have never found so young a man very interesting, before. I copy these things from a note-book he used to carry:

"'To a truly great man compliments are worthless; flattery and adulation the emptiness of folly. They may move him an instant; but his own capacity to be

6

moved by them he recognizes as a weakness, and must deplore.'

" 'I have seen men of genius lose their influence and become contemptible, and finally doubt and despise themselves, for the want of exercising judgment in their actions—trying to make opportunities to display themselves. If one will only pursue his business quietly, prosecute his studies diligently, never expend his fire on false alarms, but be observant without talking too much, opportunities frequently enough present themselves, without one's forever trying to drag them up by the locks! Nor need a man be afraid of not realizing that he has an opportunity; for the fitness of things will impress him so strongly that he cannot mistake it, and if he has prepared himself for action by study and reflection he will find himself abreast with the occasion. But one should ever feel the necessity of being unobtrusive! It is the very negative essential of positive influence.'

" How different is he from my poor father! I could love him for those last two sentences!

" Here are a few vigorous lines whose enthusiasm stirs me (he is writing of Daniel Webster):

" 'In the subtleties of metaphysics Calhoun was his superior; in that genial and hearty eloquence which at once captivates and delights us, Henry Clay was his master; in fiery and vehement partisanship Hayne surpassed him; but in dignity of port, in magnanimity, in loftiness of purpose and sublimity of imagination, no man was ever his equal except Socrates! Calhoun appealed to the understanding of men, and was their instructor—Clay appealed to their hearts, and he was their idol—Hayne appealed to their passions, and he was their leader; but Webster appealed to their imagination, and he was their hero!'

" 'Every fact contains a truth. Facts are varied; truth is always the same. Facts are forms in which truth doth express itself. Facts are new; truth is old—older than the hills, or the earth, or the sun! It antedates chaos, and is coeval with divinity, whose attribute it is!'

"I have seen in the calm attention of his eyes as he patiently considered some apparently trifling things, that very thought, 'Every fact contains a truth.'

" And—and I wonder if he has ever met his ideal woman? I read:

" ' O ideal woman, thou art clothed with modesty as with a garment ! It is an atmosphere about thee, as the lambent summer air lit by the evening star. Thou hast it as a flower its sweet perfume—as the rose its wondrous odor, or the violet its dreamy scent. It is a principle of grace that speaks in all thy actions : that fires the blush that burns upon thy cheek, and draws about thy softest glances the fringed curtains of the eyes.'

" I will copy no more to night.

" It was a great confidence in him to intrust this book to me. People sometimes do trust me strangely.

" I wonder if he would tell me if he has ever been in love ?

" 2d August.

" The book has told me. In a little side pocket of it I found some leaves cut out from the body of its pages, as if to throw them away ; and then, as if repenting of the intention to bestow a half-confidence, they are put back again into this little place at the side. Across the outside leaf is scrawled a line of Swinburne's —this :

" ' **Time turns the old days to derision.**'

Within are verses. Their orderly connection is more recent than the poems, and their title, as a whole, is newly written. As they stand, they are five little poems called

A LOVER'S MOODS.

I.

" ' Like sunshine enter, O bright Love, my mind,
    Gloomy and dark as caverns of the wind;
    There shall what gems soever thou may'st light
    Resplendent in thy presence flash so bright,
    That all the world, though it be lit by me,
    Still for the cause shall ever turn to thee !'

Charming ! she was to be his inspiration, then ?

II.

" ' My soul is a lake;
        My love is a star;
    When on me divinely
        She shines from far,
    Calm the lake's surface,
        Serene are its deeps,
    While round it unheeded
        The dark shade sleeps.

" ' Her message is the zephyr
        With sweetest perfume fraught;
    Her smile the softest radiance
        Upon its surface caught.

The day withdraws too slowly,
But in its fading light
The lake glows, longing only
For shadow, silence, night!

" ' Break forth in thy beauty,
O radiant star!
Rest, rest on my bosom
Thy smile from afar.
Sweet the wave's ripplings wake,
Joyous and low
When lit with thy brightness
Its murmuring flow !'

There's music and fancy in this : but *was* it love ?

III.

" ' By me, I'll swear, nor ode, nor verse,
Henceforth shall woman's charms rehearse!
Sapphic odes and metric lays,
Wreaths of flowers, crowns of bays,
All honors of poetic art
Are here discarded by my heart;
This song's the last in beauty's praise—
Long life be hers, and happy days.'

What called forth that, I wonder ?

IV.

" ' And yet I know—for I have seen—
How small a space there lies between
The memory of some rapturous kiss,
And fixed resolves—e'en such as this!'

Afterthought! But come—he has begun to laugh at himself, and to name a 'rapturous kiss' lightly—there is hope for him.

v.

" ' Alas! and who shall say:
" I've done with love,
Nor tears nor laughter gay
My mind can move:
Nor can all witcheries
Of coquettish art,
Nor beauty's sweetes. treacheries
Beguile my heart "?
Lo ! still rebellious ocean, well I ween,
Obedience yields, though to a faithless queen.'

This is very pretty, but I should not like a man to write it of me, were he my lover!

"Well! In glancing back to see if this is correctly copied, I find I have treated these poems in a remarkable manner. Pray, Miss Alwyn, are these literary criticisms so interspersed among these stanzas? Ah! Drosée, Drosée, what are you thinking of? What are you forgetting?

" *It is impossible.*

"Even if he loved me—as he does not—*impossible.*

“ August 3d.

“ I have had a strange conversation with Fanny Fielding. I shall try to write down all that we said, each of us.

“ Aunt Mary, who has paid her usual summer visit to her father-in-law’s country house, has invited one of us girls to go with her to the White Mountains. Uncle Adrian is going, too, and leave Louis to attend to his business alone this year.

“ ‘ Jo is going to insist on my accepting it,’ I said to Fanny. ‘ But I don’t think I shall, though she says it is my turn. I may, though.’

Then without more ado Fanny Fielding turned abruptly to me and said :

“ ‘ Drosée, what are you going to do with Wilmer ? I believe that he loves you. I know it ; he told me so long ago.’

“ ‘ Fanny,’ said I, lightly, ‘ don’t try to be a matchmaker, dear. You’ll spoil the nicest, most comfortable, reliable friend I possess, if you take a notion like that. I won’t have it, my dear, and there’s an end on’t. I won’t be made love to—do you hear ?’

“ ‘ Drosée,’ she said, with a sudden and unexpected

seriousness in her manner, 'if I believed that you would never marry, I should be the most unhappy woman alive. I should feel that my wicked folly had spoiled your life; that I had broken your one dream, and that you——'

" 'Hush!' I said. 'If I had truly loved my *fiancé*, do you think that I could not have forgiven him? I could forgive—anything—to a man who had entirely won me! He told me a falsehood about his former engagement to you; he paid you, when a married woman, attentions which might possibly have compromised you; he was cruel to you and false to me— *but what of that? if I had loved him!'*

" 'He was the most elegant and captivating gentleman I have ever known,' Fanny slowly said. *I* know how charmingly he can befool both girl and woman! When I was engaged to him—well, I have never loved since as I did then, and though he left me, and I married Henry in a fit of pique, and tried to forget him, his memory haunted me through nearly fifteen years, and until two years ago he was never truly wrenched from my heart. And you, whom he truly loved—*you* did not love him at all? It is hard to believe!'

6*

" 'I can scarcely understand my own conduct,' I replied to her. 'I did admire him; I believed him good and refined; he was rich, he was handsome, he had ready and graceful manners; I admit all that. He seemed to me the best of our circle, and was considered a catch, a little elderly, fastidious, and difficult. Of course his devotion, which made a belle of me, flattered me immensely. The worst of it is, you know, that girls like to have things happen. I had made up my mind then to love and be married some day; and with this foreordained and expected, I mistook the fluttering of vanity for the flutter of love. I believe that many girls marry on just so shallow and fleeting a fancy, and think that they know what love is! Thank Heaven, I escaped!'

" 'And yet'—went on this irrational woman, 'if you and I had never met at Newport, and you had never heard the gossip about us, and had not, unlike any other woman, taken my part and saved me from myself by the infectious power of your courage and candor—if this had not come to pass, my dear, you would be by this time nearly two years married to one of the "ornaments of society," and have queened it as the prettiest and wisest young matron of them all.'

" I think I must have shuddered even as she uttered these last words fondly.

" ' I thank heaven I was fair to you, and am a free woman,' I said; ' I don't wholly regret that experience, after all, though once I did, bitterly. It has set me to live a more calm and unexpectant life, looking for changes from within, not without. But I am thankful to believe that Jo will never go through this. If she once falls in love, it will be for once and all, for life or death. I shall never see her resign herself to a series of "engagements," as other girls have done; never have her know—bless her !—the cheap, the " handled," the *light* feeling of a woman who has been gracious to more than one lover !'

" ' Drosée, I am not thinking of Jo's future love-affairs,' Fanny broke in, impetuously, ' I am thinking of *yours !* You have made one mistake——'

" ' And I shall not repeat it !' I said, hotly, smarting yet with the revived sting of that old hurt, ' never name me "love" again !'

" And it was not until after I left her that I began to realize what she had told me.

" She had no right to betray his confidence in order to gratify herself. It was unjust to him to tell me he had said that.

" He has given me no sign of loving me. He is proud and reserved, and he would never offer his love to a woman whose heart he knew so little. Our acquaintance has had in it little of the sentimental. He is apparently as likely to be Jo's lover as mine.

" But he is wonderful! He makes me happier, clearer-headed, more high-minded, more sincere, by his very presence. I would be a better woman with him than without him.

" I prefer him to any man I ever knew. I admire and trust him. But do I love him ?

" I will not if I can help it !

" 6th August.

" I have done a strange thing. Yet not so strange ; for lately we have chanced to be so much together that it is as if we had known each other a long time. But now I have given Mr. Wilmer my confidence as to things I have never named to any other person since I have been a woman grown. I have told him about my mother. It is a sad and shameful story. I did not doubt but that it was new to him. When I had finished, he said gently, ' I can never tell you how I appreciate your confiding in me ; some part of this I had indeed heard——'

" ' It is known even in Fairvalley, then ?' I ejaculated.

" ' No—do not be disquieted. Your father is generally looked upon here as a widower,' he said. ' I did not hear this from any chance gossip. I would not have listened to it from a malicious tongue.'

" ' It was—Fanny, then ?'

" ' You are not displeased ?'

" ' Not at all. She is an honest woman !' I was glad Fanny had not attempted to make him think well of me in ignorance of our family disaster.

" ' It was Fanny,' he acknowledged.

" ' And from the first you have known,' I began.

" ' I have known for some time,' he said, with great gentleness, ' of this loss and grief of yours. It has invested you and your sister with a new sacredness in

my eyes. Should you think it could do anything
else ?'

"His tone, and look, and words moved me strongly.
The tears rushed to my eyes. He bent his head, and I
felt his lips touch my hand. Then we both started
apart; there were steps in the hall, and in another moment Jo came into the parlor. Mr. Wilmer had risen.
Dark as he was, he had colored deeply, and looked embarrassed. Jo was all unsuspicious. She said, laughingly :

" ' It is too bad for you to have started to go just as
I came in. I have scarcely seen you lately, Mr. Wilmer. Sit down again, and tell me what you are going
to say about Landor in your essay—don't you wish you
were reader instead ?'

" ' No, for I shall hear your sister read,' he said.

" He staid only a few minutes longer, laughing and
talking with Jo. They have become friends enough
to quarrel—Jo's surest sign of favor. They discourse
like children together; and grave and serious as he may
be the instant we are alone, when she comes in he is
wonderfully transformed, and is like a boy, ready for
mischief and nonsense.

'When he left—and all this time he had not once looked me in the face—he bowed to us both; but his face was grave and his eyes lowered when he turned to me. There is something more winning in his silent deference than in another's most eloquent praise.

"8th August.

"Fanny asked me to spend the day with her yesterday, and Mr. Wilmer was invited to tea. As it was our club night, she ought not to have had two of us to tea and not the other two; but she is willful, and a transparent little matchmaker. After early tea she soon managed to desert us, we having gone out with her on the lawn. After she had left us, we walked on together, slowly, down the path through the shrubbery, across the little rustic bridge over the smoothly winding stream, and over to the shady avenue under the elms.

"'Had you not some difficulty in selecting a reading for to-night?' he asked.

"'The embarrassment of riches,' I answered. 'There was a world of fine writing before me, and whether in poetry or prose Landor displays more brilliant, fanciful, and varied powers it is hard enough to tell.'

" ' You should read more than one selection,' he suggested. 'Indeed, one is sure to be too short. He is as dainty and light upon the wing as a butterfly, and takes very brief, though sometimes exquisitely loitering, flights. Each color and odor attracts him, and he flutters past us to another just as we are fascinated in watching him hover about one near at hand.'

" This simile the prodigal young man wasted on me! I listened for it, but heard not a trace of it in the fine essay he read later in the evening; I answered,

" 'And that is why, though he often piques, he never tires his readers. "As temperate as a butterfly"—he deserves George Eliot's graceful phrase.'

" ' And so you have selected more than one passage ?'

" 'I lingered lovingly over some of the "imaginary conversations," which were quite long enough; but in a mere one of them he was not sufficiently represented in his variety : I collated some of his Hellenics—"Iphigenia," and " The Shades of Agamemnon and Iphigenia," with the " Death of Clytemnestra " and the "Madness of Orestes ;" I am not sure but I would have done best to decide on these; they seem to me the most moving and powerful of all his poems. But I decided at last on some of the letters of Pericles and Aspasia, as showing forth alike wit, tenderness, fancy, and power. When I read them, I hope you will think the choice made with discretion.'

"'I am sure I shall," he said; 'your taste, like yourself, is beyond cavil; beyond praise, I might say, if I dared to speak my mind.'

"He spoke with that air of deliberate reflection and gravity which always flavors his rare compliments, and though they may be extravagant one can scarcely presume to laugh at him, so earnest and dignified is he when he thus addresses one.

"It is in this way he puts me on my good behavior. I feel when I am with Mr. Wilmer as if I were in the best of good company, and am in much such a mood at times as I should be in if mingling with those I have known and loved in books—the wise and fine gentlemen of a past time—the wits, and statesmen and philosophers, the choice society of Queen Elizabeth's or Queen Anne's reign. The more I compare him with other men the more unusual I find him in every way.

"We went on walking in the avenue and talking for some time. There was nothing which he said or did that was precisely lover-like; and yet, he could not have said to *two* women some of the things he has said to me; and to me, although he is but my friend, he is fast becoming more near and dear than any other.

"When we were summoned back to the house by a message from Fanny, Dr. Stark had come, but without Jo. He had called for us, but he said that Louis Seaford was there, and that Jo had staid at home to entertain him.

"Mr. Wilmer looked perturbed; and Dr. Stark, who was talking to me, looked up and said, teasingly:

"'Are all of us quite unequal to the task of making you forget this disappointment?'

"Mr. Wilmer did not answer. When he is displeased I have noticed that he is immovably silent.

"The evening passed off pleasantly enough, and when Mr. Wilmer and I, who had agreed to walk home together, started, Dr. Stark naturally joined us. As he called out,

"'Hold, Wilmer, I'm coming,' Mr. Wilmer said under his breath, 'As I expected!' But though the frown re-visited his face he responded readily with an apt quotation:

> "'Thou canst not come too soon; and I can wait
> If thou come late.'

"Both left me at the door, and I came up here and have been scribbling ever since. Louis and Jo had left the parlor empty and gone for a walk. There was a note for me on the table by the ice-pitcher, in Aunt Mary's hand. She wants us to decide at once which will go with her, and come up to New York at the end of the week. Jo must go. I do not care for the trip at all. I suppose Louis came down to see about it. It is time those children had returned. When I hear their voices I shall go down-stairs. It is a lovely night for a walk. I should have enjoyed mine more—but that is ungrateful to a true and tried old friend!

"I must face this matter out sometime. Why not to-night?

"I will not say that Mr. Wilmer loves me—yet. It is perhaps vain in me to think that this rare and wonderful man, so strangely compounded of power and gentleness, could ever choose me—love me. But—it is dishonest in me to deny an influence over him which I feel myself to possess. If I ever tried to please, to conquer, to use those about me, I have usually succeeded. He is stronger, finer, better—but he cares for me enough for me to know that he will care for me more, if I will. Dare I?

"I am not wicked enough to be willing to hurt him. If I am willing to be loved by him—and that indeed I cannot deny that I am; I would be proud and glad of his love—I ought to be willing to give the rein to my own emotions, and to let my love go out to him in return. If I am not willing for this—it is the only right and fair and wise thing to do, to recognize possibilities and leave him to himself.

"I know that many a woman would shut her eyes, bid chance direct her, and let any man—the wiser the better—meet his doom, fall a victim to her 'modesty' and 'innocence,'—so-called—to her pride and folly!

"I cannot. I always think—I always reflect. It is a curse of mine.

"He is so noble—I cannot—

"I hear voices. I must go!

"9th August.

"As Mr. Wilmer came by this morning he stopped and came in. He brought me the latest number of Harper's, in which we are reading Daniel Deronda; and a single stalk of tuberoses, thickly blooming with those chaste and waxen little lilies whose perfume he knows I delight in. He is obliged to stay in the city to night, he told me. To-morrow night, might he come and hear what I thought of this number?

"When he had shaken hands and gone I opened the magazine. Daniel Deronda he had read and marked. The first sentence I read therein was this, scored by a pencil: 'Sometimes, with a sweet irresistible hopeful-ness that the very best of human possibilities might befall him—the blending of a complete personal love in one current with a larger duty.' He knew, when he marked it, that my eye would rest on this.

"I will wait. My life is no longer my own to make. It *is* 'the very best of all human possibilities,'—'a com-plete personal love'—if it is offered me by a man who would not hinder but help me to do my duty, live my life, develop the best of me—if, I say, it is offered me. There is a 'sweet, irresistible hopefulness' that it may be!

"I blush at my own meekness—at my own daring. I cannot look myself in the face after writing such words as these. I will write no more!

" Night.

"———Oh, I started to put into words what has just come to me. But not now. I cannot now! To-morrow I *must* face it. Oh, Jo, my one little sister! To-morrow will do to think. To-night I can only feel, and hide what I am feeling!

"10th August. Afternoon.

" 'Surrender and denial of all that is self.'

" How often have I set those words before me, and marked with them the height I wished to attain! How often have I said to myself that all personal and selfish joy is petty, and the end of such anticipations disappointment? That the only rational life is that of the soul—which neither fears nor hopes for its own happiness, but finds virtue enough?

"The test of all my theories of life has been applied; the trial of my deepest philosophy is upon me!

Can I deny my personal desires, deny my selfish longing, and cheerfully become one of the many women
who live without deep joys?

"To give up happiness—surely for Jo's sake I could
do that! But it is not happiness alone I give up with
Mr. Wilmer. He does not mean simply joy to me:
he means—life. The best possible life I could live.
His presence is not delight only; it is thought, animation, pure aspiration, love of good, strength against
evil. To give him up is to give up some inspiration
for soul and spirit, without which I shall never fully
live. It is to be an undeveloped nature. He is—life!

"I had just begun to know this: to see how he had,
by his pure and wise companionship, raised my existence to a higher level. I had never fully lived. I
now found there were stirring in me a hundred
delicate activities new to me as he.—I suppose if I
were dying I should analyze my sensations!—This is
vain.

"Jo urged me, before Louis left, to say that I would
take the trip Aunt Mary offered to one of us. Louis,
too, privately informed me that he thought his mother
would rather have me; but I told him I thought it

would have to be Jo this time; I would write to Aun
Mary ; and so he left, uncertain.

"Yesterday afternoon Jo came and stood before me
pale and palpitating, but determined. I had neve
seen just such a look on her fair young face.

" 'Drosée! I wish, seriously and—selfishly—not to
go away. It is not for your sake I am putting the trip
aside. Honestly, I do not want to go. Please make
up your mind to that. I am not to be forced to go.'

"I looked at her with astonishment.

" 'Forced? My dear child, I never thought of
such a thing! If you don't want to go, you need not
But it will be a delightful trip, and I thought you were
refusing it for my sake, with your usual unselfishness.

" 'It is not that,' said Jo, a little unsteadily. Then
she flung herself on her knees beside me and hid her
face on my breast.

" 'I am such a fool—I would not have told you i
you could only have seen for yourself—but I—I like
Fairvalley—and *he* will be here and not there—an
here I should be happy, and there I shouldn't !'

" 'Jo!' I said, after an instant's pause, and as quiet
as I could, 'tell me fairly. Can it be that you love—

There was no need of the name between us. Her arm tightened about my neck, and my heart seemed to break within me, as she spoke.

" ' I can't help it!' she said, in a muffled voice. ' I have always laughed at him, and quarreled with him, and tried to stave him off in every way. And all the time he was making me love him in spite of myself. And when it comes to choosing between all these weeks with him or without him—Drosée, why should I be such a fool as to go and be wretched?'

"She moved to lift her head, and I stooped hastily and put my cheek against hers, and kissed her, for I could not speak. She lay against my breast, and I looked down at her. There were tears beneath her shut lashes, and her lips looked soft and tremulous. There was a pathos in Jo's quiet, childish beauty that wrung my heart. She turned and hid her face again, asking, ' Are you sorry? If it had been any one else—but you know how good he is! and father—father has always *angled* for him, because he is to be rich—that was a great objection ——'

" ' Hush, hush, Jo!' I said (to what eligible man that ever came near us was *not* father painfully

7

cordial?). ‘If he loves you, love him truly. But be sure he loves you well.’

“She lifted her head; her eyes were brave and a little indignant, but she smiled faintly.

“‘Loves me?’ she said, ‘If he does not, he —— but give me these three weeks, Drosée, and I’ll tell you for true!’

“‘You shall stay in Fairvalley,’ I said.

“‘And will you go to Aunt Mary to-morrow or Saturday?’

“‘I have not said that I should go at all,’ I answered, rising. ‘Do not let us talk of that any more to-day,’ and so I left her.

“But I ought to go! If he has been at all undecided between us—if it be possible—I ought to go, if I would give Jo a fair chance. It is natural that he should love her! He has been to me a friend. We accord. We like to think over things together. He may approve of me: but yet love Jo! Her sweet, flashing, tempting beauty, her gayety and youth, her wit and piety—Jo is better than I. I am elder, paler, with less variety and less goodness. Yet, if it be true—as Fanny said—as I have sometimes felt—that he is attracted by me, the only thing for me to do is to remove my influence from him, and leave Jo's beauty and excellence to work, with unrivaled force, their natural effect upon him.

" For me, my philosophy has been ' Virtue is enough.'

"My religion has been to love God. I have desired to be truly religious and wise.

"Then must I now renounce my desire of love. Amen."

When Drosée had finished this last line she dropped her pen, and sat silently, with her face looking heavenward. The evening sky was bright with sunset still. She sat moveless for many minutes. Her face was quite calm but pale. She did not stir until she heard a step on the stair; then rising hastily she closed the book before her as Jo entered. This is the way a woman slurs over a tragic mood.

" Jo! shall I take your trunk or mine? And do you think I'll have any use for that buff lawn?"

" Sensible girl! You have made up your mind to enjoy yourself," Jo said, and sat down on the bed to consider Drosée's queries.

"You are going away to-morrow?" Wilmer asks, that night, in a low, troubled voice. He has come to spend the appointed evening with Drosée, but when he enters finds Mr. and Mrs. Fielding before him, Drosée having dispatched a request to her friend to come and spend her "last evening in Fairvalley" with her. There is to be no *tête-à-tête* over that book to-night, she has resolved.

Wilmer is informed of the meaning of his cousin's visit. His cousin is at the little cottage piano now, playing brilliant and noisy music. Mr. Fielding and Jo are by the table, and Mr. Alwyn, who has called Drosée aside a moment, now leaves her and joins them. Fanny gives Wilmer a quick look, and he is not slow to perceive his opportunity. He joins Drosée before she can leave the window.

"Yes, it is sudden—to me. But I found all my plans made for me yesterday," she answers, smiling and outwardly calm.

"You are going to the Crawford House," Wilmer says. "My grandfather happens to be there, and my grandmother—my only near relatives. May I write to them to call upon you and Mrs. Seaford?"

"I should be very much gratified; but is it not strange you never told me where they were before?"

"Their whereabouts has not particularly interested me till now," he answers, with the ghost of a smile. "But *now*, I may run up to see them soon. May I?"

A flash of some vivid emotion—surprise, as Wilmer interpreted it—passed over her face.

"You should not ask *me*," she faltered.

"Excuse me. I will come without your permission. Yet had you bid me come I should not have presumed to hope too much from it."

The gentle, deferential, manly tone carried with it a thrill so sharp as to be near a pang; then Drosée lifted her eyes, but dropped them suddenly, answering coldly:

"Do not come because of my being there, please."

Not another word was said. Wilmer's lips tightened, and his eyelids contracted slightly—it was his only betrayal of pain. Drosée could scarcely have been paler, but she looked calm, cold and serene. She turned her head and listened to the music.

Fanny had begun to sing. The sweet invitation of

the song went through and through Drosée's soul in shuddering strains—

"Ernani, Ernani, fly with me!"

Drosée never afterwards could listen calmly to that song.

When it was done, she rose and joined her friend. Wilmer rose too, and stood with bent head for her to pass. He left immediately after the Fieldings took leave, without other word to Drosée than "Good-bye," as he took and then relinquished rather slowly her small, cold hand.

Thus briefly and significantly was the hard word spoken.

CHAPTER VI.

"I notice fickleness of weather
  In that strange climate of the heart:
People forget love when together—
  I think we won't do worse apart."—W. D. HOWELLS.

DROSÉE is far away. Mr. Alwyn has gone in to New York to make some final arrangements with the unwary purchaser of the play he has been writing all summer, and which he has now sold—by a wonderful chance—for a moderate sum. He is much elated by this small triumph, boasts noisily about his "new play," and has asked Miss Ball to go in to the city with his daughters and himself to see it acted on the great "first night." Miss Ball is extremely flattered; she believes Mr. Alwyn, who is the only literary man she has ever known, to be one of the greatest modern authors, taking him at his own price with a simple loyalty of belief which has grown to be immensely pleasing and soothing to this baffled genius; for egregiously vain as the man is, he is naturally keenly stung by the fact sometimes thrust upon him, that he is lightly esteemed. Miss Ball's admiration of him is sincere, ignorant, and sweet. Mr. Alwyn is thinking much of Miss Ball in these days, and rating her charms and abilities higher and higher as she more and more falls under his influence.

Ignorant of this, Jo has been living a happy life for these past two weeks. Louis Seaford, whom she has known ever since she was a baby, and he was a boy in round jackets, has come out to the Fairvalley House, and goes in and out to his business every day. It is the only change of air he can make this summer, he says, " since the governor has up and taken to himself a holiday."

" You know, Louis, I think—hard as it is to believe—" Jo says, demurely, as she and Louis sit in the front piazza in the yellow moonlight of a September night, alone—for Mr. Alwyn has not yet returned from New York—"I think you must have come to be some sort of a comfort to Uncle Adrian at last! It is the first time in ages that he has ever left his business and taken a summer holiday; *you* used to go every summer, and let him fag it out alone."

"Yes, it's pleasant to remember. Thank you for reminding me," Louis says, with rather a vicious grip of his teeth on his cigar. His blonde, manly young face, and his usually gay and even mischievous eyes are cloudy enough now. The dimple fades in Jo's cheek.

"I suppose I 'nag' a good deal, do I, Lou?" she says, half coaxingly.

Louis moves his chair a half inch nearer.

"Jo," he says, seriously, "I have a good deal to thank you for, you know, in just this way. You have always been so truthful, so keen, so just, in your scorn of me—"

"Scorn, Louis?"

"Yes, Jo. You fairly despised me after I left college, for a year or so. And it used to stay by me—that there was one girl I couldn't coax, or wheedle, or laugh at, or—however I tried—please, while I went dilly-dallying along, trying to play the brilliant, idle young beau. You even mocked at my mustache, Jo, when its length was the pride of my young life."

The laugh returns to his grave blue eyes now. Jo

7*

feels more at ease. I think it is Jo moves her chair a little nearer this time.

Louis throws away his cigar. He puts his hand on Jo's, which is in her lap; and Jo allows him—he is her cousin, she argues—to slip his fingers around and beneath it, and inclose that soft, small hand in his own.

"Do you remember the day in the Park, Jo?" he asks, in a low tone.

"I said some dreadful things to you, I remember," Jo says softly, "I did not mean them—all—Louis."

"You told me I had no right to call myself a man, unless I could do a man's work; and no right to talk of love, until I could prove that I knew of any better sort than self-love."

"Louis," Jo says, quickly, "do not recall all our old quarrels. I used to be a regular vixen, and fancy I was preaching. I did not like your ways, Louis—but I always liked you!"

"What did you like in me, Jo? You never mentioned anything," Louis observes, demurely. Jo shoots a keen side glance at him, and then replies frankly:

"I liked you because you had some sense. You could argue well, when you chose; you read books worth reading; you did not affect to be anything particular, but you were always on a level with the best men and women who came to the house, and up to the times in every way. How you kept up, I couldn't guess; but somehow you knew all about everything Drosée and I cared for. I liked that. I hate a fool!"

"Ye gods! So you liked me because I wasn't a fool?"

"I liked you because you were a reader and a thinker, and had more brains than any other young fellow I knew," Jo says earnestly. "And—I—always thought—you had a respect for religion," she adds, softly. "You never used your wit to ridicule anything sacred in the eyes of your fellow-men. Ah! if you knew how detestable Guy Farnham made himself, just that way."

"I never see Guy now," Louis replies quietly. "Jo, I begin to have some hopes that you did not use to quite hate me. Was—was there *any* thing else you liked in me, dear?"

They are very close together, now. Louis bends toward her.

"I—I always thought you handsome, Louis," Jo tu.ters.

It is too much; Louis gives a little short, happy laugh, and catches Jo in his arms.

"You dear, blessed, absurd little Josephus!" he exclaims softly. "And I—Jo, I always thought you the prettiest, sweetest, best, and most impossible little woman in this world; but I have meant, ever since that day in the Park, to have you at last!"

"But you haven't got me!" Jo says, struggling.

"Yes, I have, my darling!" Louis answers, holding her fast; and, taking her unawares, he kisses her as he has never before, in all their days as cousins, kissed those tender lips.

Jo buries her face in his collar an instant after that and then she sits up as straight as his arms permit.

"Please to let me go," she says, in a low, displeased voice.

"My little Jo, have I offended you?" Louis asks, releasing her. Jo stands up. She is trembling slightly. She is quite pale.

"You had no right to treat me so," she says, in a strange, hard tone.

Louis rises also.

"Not unless you give me the right, Jo," he answers, gravely, tenderly. "But I thought you would, my—Jo. I thought you would be my wife, darling. I have had this hope always before me. I—all these days we have been so happy together, Jo; I have been watching your face every hour we were together; sometimes the fulfillment of all my expectation seemed so near that I thought I could only put out my arms, and clasp it to me forever."

"You have thought I loved you—more than a cousin —all this time?"

"I have hoped so—lately—Jo, you do!"

These three words, his sudden step towards her, ruin all his chance. Jo's pride flames up in a breath.

"I do not!" she ejaculates, a burning blush rushing over her fair face and body, and the lie uttering itself unawares in her tremor of maiden shame.

Louis steps back. He looks at her with a strange, severe expression in his eyes.

"Jo, are you a flirt?" he asks. "Would you flirt even with—me? You have given me every reason of late to believe that you would accept me; you have been another woman from the one I loved last year. You have behaved as if you loved me, Jo."

"Go away, Louis," Jo says, in a strangely suppressed voice. "I will not listen to you any longer. I never threw myself at any man as you assert. I never tried to make you think I loved you. Cophetua as you are, the beggar-maid cannot make up her mind to royal amenities."

And without another word Jo steps within the open door and shuts it swiftly. The latch snaps; the door is locked to all but a night-key, and Louis stands aghast and motionless.

Presently he throws himself into one of the empty chairs, and leans his handsome head upon his arm, thrown along the piazza rail.

"My dear, proud, tender little love!" he says, under his breath. "I have gone about it clumsily. My poor, proud little Jo! Cophetua, indeed! She thought I seemed too sure of her!"

He lifts his face again.

"Bless her soul! I would have gone on my knees to her, if I had only known. What a clumsy, cruel, foolish way to approach a grave, serious-hearted, intense little woman! Anybody who only knew her in her lightest moods might have made such a blunder. I'll see her and apologize."

He starts up: he goes to the door. He knocks gently; there is no answer. He steps off the piazza and walks around to the side window on the noiseless turf, and looks into the parlor. There is the glimmer of white in the corner where the sofa is.

"Jo," he says. No answer—no sound.

"Jo, take pity on me: speak to me just once. I can't go."

The moonlight streams into the room, and outlines his head and shoulders in shadow on the floor. The waving shadow of the branch of a leafy tree flutters on the carpet. The room is all dark, except for this broken patch of light.

"Jo! Sweetheart! Jo, do not make me so miserable, when a word would help me so?"

He fancies there is a movement—a sob. Or is it but the wind?

He is tall, lithe, active. He makes a leap, upon the window-sill, and enters the room. In the darkness he goes blundering across to the sofa. He puts out his hand, and touches the white shape. It is nothing but a long white tidy neatly pinned along the back of the sofa.

Of all the men who have inveighed against these innocent products of feminine idleness, Louis is one of the most sincere.

He turns away, and calling " Jo " still softly and in vain, opens the door into the hall. He wanders through all of the down-stairs rooms; but Jo is in none of them. For a moment he is tempted to rush up-stairs and beat a tattoo on her door as he used to in his school-boy days; but he dares not. Jo is not to be approached with the lightest assumption of cousinly familiarity; he must come a-wooing with all the deference of a strange lover, he perceives at last. He loves her better already for this very distance she has put between them. He sits down in an easy-chair in the dining-room, his head between his hands, and thinks some very gentle and reverential thoughts of her whom he has loved so long. He recalls with new force her beauty—her spirit—her goodness—her truth —her glimpses of rare lovingness. Never in his life has Louis so clearly understood how he loves his cousin. Could Jo have come to him then, he would have wooed her with a reverential tenderness that would have satisfied her that she was loved as deeply and purely as she desired.

The stillness grew around the silent young man; the unquiet shadows and changing lights out of doors were banished from this dark room; he was fallen into deep thought, and marked neither the flight of time, nor the faint sound of a latch-key which was softly fitted in the lock of the front door, about midnight. Rousing suddenly with the sense of a presence in the room—for Mr. Alwyn had entered the dining-room to get a glass of water—he rose to his feet, stammering, " Sir."

"Ow! Oh! Get!" roared Mr. Alwyn, darting backward, almost deprived of the power of speech by fright. And then, recovering himself by an effort, he yelled in terror:

" Thieves! Help! Murder! Jemima!" and beat the air with his cane in a perfect panic.

Louis attempted to speak, but his laughter overcame him; and suddenly it occurred to him that he could give no very rational account of his presence, and had best use his chance to escape. Parrying a stroke of Mr. Alwyn's cane by a light blow that sent his uncle's arm up, he dashed by him, leaped out of the open parlor window, snatched his hat from the piazza steps, and in half a minute had cleared the grounds and was walking leisurely towards his hotel, laughing to himself in a strangely cheerful manner for a discarded lover.

Next morning Louis came by the cottage on his way, apparently, to take an earlier train to the city than usual; but, as if thinking better of it, paused, opened the gate, and entered. Mr. Alwyn was upon the front porch, smoking.

"Good morning, good morning," the uncle said, with his usual heartiness of welcome to this young man. "Heard of the excitement, I suppose? I'm quite knocked up, I assure you. The most astonishing thing in life how the fellow got away. I've marked him, though—he's got a mark he'll carry for life, I'll be bound."

"How was it, sir?"

"I came in about midnight—been to New York to see some actors, old chums of mine, and had a pleasant evening—couldn't get away from them, in fact—and coming in quietly and entering the dining-room, I found a tall fellow in a mask in the very act of rifling the sideboard of the silver—careless of the girls to leave it there, but they won't carry it up to their room at night to save me! I gave one jump at the fellow, and struck a blow with my cane—he dodged me, and I chased him around the room, and hit him one sounding blow. He gave a groan, and then rushed at me, nearly disabled my arm, and before I knew what had hit me, he had gone. I roused the house, and Jo and the girl helped me light it up, and look in every nook and corner of it. We found the parlor window wide open, and I suppose he got in that way. I never had a thing give me such a shock in my life."

"Where is Jo? Was she much alarmed?" Louis asked, with genuine concern.

"She was, at first, but when we discovered no one, she went back to bed, and she has not come down yet."

"Can Jemima be sent up to see how she is?"

"I'll go myself," Mr. Alwyn answered, rising. It

dawned pleasantly upon him that Louis seemed very much interested in Jo's health.

- "Jo!" he shouted at the foot of the stairs.

"Coming!" answered Jo's clear voice; and in another minute she came down the stair.

"Louis is on the porch; come out," said Mr. Alwyn. Jo stood still. Louis arose from the steps where he had seated himself, and came in.

"Good morning," said Jo, very coldly.

"Good morning," said Louis, gently. His eyes sought hers with an entreaty in them.

"I have been telling Louis about the robbery attempted here last night," Mr. Alwyn said. Jo flushed, and gave Louis a strange look.

"If it had not been for my opportune return, we shouldn't have had a spoon to eat breakfast with," went on Mr. Alwyn. "I only wish I had trapped the rogue. But he'll remember me, I imagine, to the last day he lives. I hear that cane go co-thump on his ugly pate this minute!"

Louis' eyes twinkled in spite of himself. Jo looked at him again, half apprehensively, half indignantly.

Mr. Alwyn puffed out his chest, and nodded. It was almost too much, but Louis did not give way.

"Well, I'm glad you escaped so lightly," he said, with a curious quiver in his voice. "I must go on, I believe. Jo—will you just walk to the gate with me? Good morning, sir."

"Wait a minute, Louis, I'll walk with you. I'm going in on this train too," said Mr. Alwyn, taking his hat from the peg. And then, remembering that he was probably standing in Jo's light by this offer, he attempted to atone by saying, "And you must come home with me this evening and take tea."

They walked away together, and Louis carried a heavy heart. Jo had never in her life looked so gravely and coldly at him—never in her life given him so lifeless a hand as that he touched at good-bye.

Louis did not come to tea with Mr. Alwyn. He concluded that he should only offend Jo by treating her as usual, and find the meal an awkward one. And so Jo, in her pale-blue muslin, coming down to meet her father at tea-time, with a fitful color coming and going in her cheek, and her coldness melting at the prospect of seeing Louis again, was disappointed and hardened again.   She was a very snow-maiden when he came in at the gate an hour after tea.   But—she was alone.

"Good evening, Jo," Louis said, offering to take her little hand.

"Good evening," said Jo, plucking a yellow leaf from the rose-vine.

"Were you much alarmed last night?" Louis asked, sitting down on the steps at her feet.

"Not at all," said Jo, coldly.   "I knew it was you."

"You *did?*   Well, of all things. And you wouldn't tell on me!"

Jo said nothing, but blushed hotly.

"How did you know, Josephus?" said Louis, gently, leaning forward.

"I found the flower I had put in your button-hole on the dining-room floor," said Jo, rather bitterly. She was not candid enough to say that she had watched at her window to see him go; had lingered there, fancying him gone, and been miserable a couple of hours; and that when her father's shouts alarmed the house, and she started up, she had stopped to see who dashed by the piazza and out of the gate, and had known his figure and his laugh as he passed the fence.

"You got in at the parlor window, I suppose," she added.

"Do ycu know whom I came to look for?" he asked.

"I don't know why you should have *staid*."

"I staid—because I could not bear to go away; because I loved you so that it was hard to leave the house you were in, Jo."

That said, Jo melted. The color burned hotter and redder on her cheek. Louis saw it.

"And when your father came in, I was lost in thoughts of you, Jo. And—and—when he called out so I fled to escape questioning or being slain. You have no idea how he thrashed around with that stick, and how he yelled at me."

Unlucky Louis! He has done it now! Sentiment on his part is yielded one instant to a perception of the ridiculous—and sentiment on Jo's is merged in mortification and displeasure. She does not laugh. Her color fades. She rises.

"*Everything* is a subject for your mirth," she says, with a severity very like her lost mother's, had she but known it. "My father—and I—and—everything. You are the most *frivolous* man I ever knew!"

If she had called him wicked or base, the young fellow might have borne it. But *frivolous!* It carried him back to his old despised, trifling, airy days, and set him down as a spoilt and scorned mere "college boy." Jo, then, thought as slightly of him and his manliness as ever! He was hurt past cure this time.

He rose up, too. He did not say a word—Jo wished, afterwards, with an unutterable pang, that he had used but one harsh word—and looking at her half a minute, he turned, and walked unhesitatingly down the path, closed the gate, and was gone.

The next morning Jo looked for him to go by. She had passed a bad night, and there were hollows under her brown eyes. But he did not pass. At seven that morning he had received a telegram from his mother:

"Come to us immediately. Your father has had a fall, and is dangerously injured. Have telegraphed to Dr. S."

Half an hour later Louis was on his way to the White Mountains.

CHAPTER VII.

CLOUDS.

" Strange and large the world is growing ;
Speak, and tell us where we are going,
Where are we going, Rubee ?"—J. G. WHITTIER.

"I DID not consult any one, because I should have been thwarted if I had, or at least bothered," Jo observed, quietly. "But as soon as I knew that Uncle Adrian—that he—that he was *dying,*" she went on, with repressed tears, "I made up my mind. I have borne to feel that we were living on his bounty, because father—because I had to, in short. But I am not going to receive my daily bread from Louis in his turn. And besides, I want to work. Work is a great cure-all, Drosée! So I wrote to Ada Marston—you knew she married a rich old widower a year after we left school?—and I knew she would do what she could for me. Well!—It turns out that the widower himself had a *colony* of children —six—and I am to teach the four younger ones, and

8   [169]

Ada will give me three hundred dollars a year. So I'm going, Drosée, to be a governess, and *that's* the meaning of this." And Jo went on sewing buttons down the front of a new dress.

Drosée had listened quietly. She stood by the mantel-piece, leaning an elbow on it, and looking down on Jo's industrious fingers. Drosée looked no better for the trip she had taken; but then the last three weeks she had spent in nursing the dying and serving the living. She looked pale, and the delicate blue shade about her eyes was more vivid. Her lips were compressed as Jo spoke, but she gave no other sign of pain. By and by she spoke very gently.

"Have you considered, Jo, that Aunt Mary earnestly wishes one of us to make our home with her, and that in New York you would be near—a certain person—and in Philadelphia——"

"I should never see him? It is the best of reasons. Drosée, do not talk to me, in Heaven's name. You know how willful and obstinate I can be. And I tell you, once for all, that I would not for the world throw myself in his way. I could not bear it. I cannot bear to have even you refer to him in that light;

it hurts me to have you merely look at me as if you remembered that I said I loved him once. Drosée, I must go away, even from you, no matter what opposes me. *You* might understand, at least! Make it easy for me, and not hard. You have all the influence and power to decide family matters. Just say you think I ought to be let alone."

"Dear little Josephus!" Drosée said, putting her hand on Jo's cheek an instant; but Jo, pale and passive, did not respond to any hint of a caress. Drosée took her hand away, and looked out of the window. Then she said firmly, "I do understand, Jo. I will help you to go, and not let them interfere or make any disturbance. I will not even say—not even say how I shall miss you, Jo!"

Jo answered not a word. She rose, with the finished garment in her hand, kissed Drosée silently, and left the room. When she returned Drosée was still standing by the window motionless, looking out. Jo walked over to the sofa. They were in the little room which was both sitting-room and parlor.

"Sit down there, Drosée, and sing to me awhile,"

Jo asked, lying down on the sofa.   Drosee went to the piano and opened it.

" Is Dr. Stark still here ?" she asked impulsively, as her hands touched the keys.

" Yes.   He says he shall stay here all the fall," Jo answered.   " It was early in September Mr. Wilmer left, you know."

" You did not see him often before he left ?" Drosée asked, in spite of herself.

" He called only twice.   And Louis was here both times, and he did not stay long," Jo answered, a " red and restless spark " kindled upon her cheek.

Drosée's hands fell on the keys, and she began playing softly.   The belief was quite fixed in her mind, now, that Jo's love for Wilmer had gone deep, and that its disappointment was as severe as Jo's nature was serious ; " for except upon the surface, Jo's is even a graver disposition than mine," Drosée thought, silently. " I can forget grief easier.   I remember saying so once to him—and he talked Greek to me !"   A little smile revisited her cheek.   Wilmer had quoted to her— " They heal their griefs, for curable are the hearts of the noble."   Then she was penitent in an instant.

"Not that I am wiser than Jo—only she is younger; and—and it is in some sort easier for me, because it was I he could have loved."

"Why don't you sing, Drosée?" Jo asked from her sofa. And Drosée opened her music-books and sang forthwith. It was that same aria of Mendelssohn's—"O rest in the Lord: wait patiently for Him; and He shall give thee thy heart's desire."

She sang it well and earnestly. "Heart's desire"—love—or simply, virtue?

Drosée was singing: and she had made up her mind that she could resign love.

"So it is really you?" said a voice at the window.

Drosée turned from the piano: Jo sat up, and to the surprise of both, the Rev. Upton Bell was standing on the piazza.

"I heard you singing," said the visitor; "and as I found the window open I ventured to assure myself by this means that you were at home again. Mrs. Fielding told me yesterday that she did not know when you would be back."

The friendly ease of his manner was inimitable. Drosée could not help smiling to herself at the calm audacity with which this "auld acquaintance" returned to her now and then, and laid claim to the position of a friend. She had scarcely seen Mr. Bell twice since their conversation on gossip, in Mrs. Fielding's parlor.

"You are coming in, I hope?" she said smiling.

"Certainly, if I may," he replied; and stepped through the window without more ado. "Good afternoon, Miss Jo," and he offered his hand to the younger sister.

"Good afternoon," said Jo, demurely. She disliked Mr. Bell on the whole; but he was a clergyman, and Drosée tolerated him, and in indifferent matters she was usually led by her sister. Drosée shook hands with Mr. Bell also, and offered him a chair.

"Have you been having a good time?" he asked. "I mean—I beg pardon—before your trip was so unfortunately interrupted?"

"I saw some new places, and made some new acquaintances—and met some old ones too;—yes, it was quite gay with us, for a time."

"You met the Goodales again, I heard."

"Yes; I believe you knew them? Mrs. Fielding told you?"

"She read me bits of some of your letters. Miss Jo, you should have heard what your sister said about those young ladies and their parents."

" Mr. Bell!"

"I couldn't help laughing at it," he retorted cheerfully. "This was about it: 'Their mother is a saint, I understand; their father has claims to being a martyr. These very pious wives often secure that palm to their husbands, I notice!'"

"You got it by heart, I think," Drosée said smoothly, looking him in the face. "Pray, Mr. Bell, have you repeated my bit of naughtiness before?"

A sudden color rushed to the young clergyman's face. He was evidently disconcerted, but he answered truthfully:

"I think I have. I know I have, in fact. But I do not think I have injured your reputation for piety. You all in Dr. Bampfyle's church have little to lose," he added, with superb impertinence.

"I forgot to tell you, Drosée," Jo began hastily; but what she forgot was not yet to be told; voices were heard without, and upon their converse entered, without warning, Mrs. Fielding and Dr. Stark, who had met her in her pony phaeton at the gate.

"You here?" Mrs. Fielding asked brusquely, looking at Mr. Bell as she passed him. "Drosée, my dear child, I heard not two minutes ago that you were here. You have come back to us a celebrity. Let me kiss you just once, child. Here is Dr. Stark too, dying to congratulate you."

"Congratulate me on anything you can think of," Drosée said, gayly holding out her hand to her old friend. "But the best thing that has happened to me in ever so long is to see you all again."

"Drosée, I have read your novel," Mrs. Fielding went on, taking a seat near Mr. Bell, to whom she threw a smile at last. "All Fairvalley has read it, in fact. We are all in fits over it. Every one thinks you are wonderful, and half of us think you are dangerous! Oh, Drosée, I pity you!"

"Thank you. But what is the trouble? Dr. Stark —please tell me—do *you* like it?" She turned her face with some anxiety towards him.

"I think it one of the most remarkable and promising works I ever saw from a young author's pen," said Dr. Stark. "You are praised in high quarters. Have you read none of the reviews?"

"Have you not read Dr. Stark's?" Mrs. Fielding exclaimed. "He gave you more than half a column —it was two weeks ago. Every one here has seen it!"

"I have not seen many notices of it," Drosée replied quickly. "I—it came out, you know, just when my uncle was so ill. And then afterwards—really I have not looked at the papers," Drosée said simply. "I thank you, Dr. Stark. You must let me have a copy of your review of me."

"Upon my life, Drosée, here comes some one else;" glancing out of the window as the gate creaked. "This is your first afternoon at home, isn't it? Well, you are holding a levee. Here is Mrs. Estwick arrayed in purple and fine linen—Drosée—" in a quick undertone, —"I am going to stay. Be careful what you say till she's out of the house. That woman hates you. Good afternoon, Mrs. Estwick. Yes, all her friends are here to welcome her home again. Do sit here, will you not?"

"I had not heard of your return, Miss Alwyn," said Mrs. Estwick, with the calm sullenness of demeanor which that lady wore when she meant to be unpleasant. "I came to see you about a little matter of business, Miss Josephine," turning to Jo. "But I am very glad to see you, Miss Alwyn. The choir has missed your voice sadly. It is not true that you have left it permanently, I trust?"

"I shall be in my place on Sunday," Drosée answered, quietly.

"It is about your Sunday-school class I came, Miss Josephine," said Mrs. Estwick, turning to Jo again.

"I must give up my class next Sunday, Mrs. Estwick," said Jo, calmly; and the rest of the company, about to turn to each other for conversation, paused in surprise. "I am about to leave Fairvalley for several months at least."

"What is that?" asked Mrs. Fielding of Drosée.

"Jo is going away. She is going to a friend of hers in Philadelphia," began Drosée.

"To be a governess," said Jo, very clearly.

"Why, I am very sorry," said Mrs. Estwick, stammering with surprise.

"What do you mean by it, Jo?" exclaimed Mrs. Fielding abruptly.

"To amuse myself," said Jo, saucily. "Amusement is always a great consideration with me. The other reasons are really not worth mentioning."

Mrs. Fielding laughed good-naturedly, and turned back to Drosée.

"But you will stay with us, and amuse yourself writing books, I hope," she said.

"Your book is one of the most graceful utterances of modern skepticism that I ever read, Miss Drosée," said Mr. Bell, flinging the apple of discord daringly in that moment's chance silence.

"Skepticism, Mr. Bell?" said Fanny, with a sudden angry glance at him.

"Your book has attracted much attention amongst us," began Mrs. Estwick.

"The skeptics are more fortunate in their champion than the orthodox, if that be true," Dr. Stark observed, in an undertone. Drosée looked at none of the speakers. She turned her eyes on Mr. Bell with serene intrepidity.

"I am sorry, Mr. Bell, to provoke your censure," she said, with proud composure. "But really, you are not very much concerned about my fancied errors, are you ? You and I so seldom meet that it is scarcely worth while to discuss any such accusation as that you make."

" Certainly not," he retorted quickly, as Mrs. Fielding opened her lips. " If I were you, I would decline to discuss any matters of belief in Fairvalley. Your rector, Dr. Bampfyle, has just fallen into that error, and Trinity Church is in a terrible excitement—is it not, Mrs. Estwick ?"

A grim smile came over Dr. Stark's visage.

" He *will* have it," he observed dryly, to Drosée, at whose side he was. " There is going to be a battle now."

" But what is it ?" asked Drosée, aside.

" Dr. Bampfyle's sermon has been grossly exaggerated," said Mrs. Estwick, promptly. " He said no such things as his enemies declare. He preached a thoughtful, eloquent sermon upon heaven and a future life. The merest nothings have been twisted into a heretical theory as to immortality. I have it on the best authority, though I was not present that morning. I have regretted my absence ever since. Miss Jo, were *you* there ?"

"Yes," said Jo, with her usual decision. "And that was what I forgot to tell you, Drosée. Dr. Bampfyle preached a great sermon on immortal life. It was the finest sermon I ever listened to," with a defiant look at Mr. Bell.

"And perfectly orthodox?" added Mrs. Estwick, triumphantly.

"And very different from the common view of it," said Jo, relentlessly. "Dr. Bampfyle certainly does not believe in the unconditional immortality of the soul; and no more do Drosée and I."

"Oh, for goodness' sake do not let us talk theology," exclaimed Mrs. Fielding, resolutely. "It is worn threadbare in Fairvalley. It has positively been the fashion, but, thank goodness, has already become *passée*. Josephus, my dear, have I not left a book of my music here? Do help me look for it, and then I must go."

That was a bold stroke of Fanny's, and effected a general rising and movement; but Mrs. Estwick was not to be frightened by the word "*passée*."

"The difficulty is that every one seems to be trying to make the Doctor's sermon fit his or her own peculiar views," she said, not without acumen. "But Miss Josephine surprises me. People who have read your book say you have some strange ideas, Miss Alwyn. Is it true that you doubt the immortality of the soul?"

No one present knew what the answer to that would be. Mrs. Fielding devoutly hoped that Drosée would not prove heretical; Dr. Stark wondered if she would attempt a discussion; Jo believed that she would answer with her distinct belief; Mr. Bell— listened. This was what Drosée said, not without dignity:

"When I publicly express my private beliefs, Mrs. Estwick, I do it in print, that I may escape the misapprehensions which you say surround the Doctor. I decline to talk of my beliefs."

"Oh, certainly," said Mrs. Estwick, slightly confused. "I dare say your views are expressed only too clearly in your book," she added, maliciously. "Really, it takes so much time to hear what people say of it, that I haven't had a chance to read it. Good evening, Mrs. Fielding—Dr. Stark. Good evening, all of you." And Mrs. Estwick retired, rustling.

"If you are going, Mrs. Fielding—" began Mr. Bell.

"But I am *not* going, now that this woman is gone," said Fanny, very decidedly. "Do not wait for me. I am going to stay I don't know how long."

"Have I offended you, Miss Alwyn?" said Mr. Bell, advancing frankly before all the rest, and offering his hand to Drosée. "I dare say I have been very disagreeable. I beg your pardon if I have."

He looked at her with a pair of frank, honest eyes. Ill-tempered and perverse as this young man could be, there was something likeable in him, because, when all was said, he was honest. He seldom abused people behind their backs as severely as he did to their faces; and he never denied anything he had really said. His rudeness was proverbial among his acquaintances; he had so established a reputation for it, that he had become somewhat of a "privileged character" in that respect. But just at this moment he was sincerely penitent for the manner in which he had annoyed this fair young woman; the one unruly, unreliable sentiment of his life was for Drosée, and served him as a conscience just then.

When he offered her his hand, Drosée lifted her

eyes to his, and then gave him a sincere and charming smile as she placed her hand in his.

"You *have* annoyed me, but I will forgive you," she said. "You are excellent discipline, Mr. Bell. Come and try me another time, if you like."

Thus dismissed, the young clergyman took his leave, with a nod to the others, and Dr. Stark offered to follow.

"Oh, no, stay, stay!" said Mrs. Fielding urgently. "We can say what we like before *you*, Dr. Stark; and in fact you know better than any one the facts I have to set before this child. Drosée, my dear, Mr. Fielding insists on my going to our house in New York next week, and I am going to leave you with more regret than I can say. There's not a soul I shall leave behind me to stand your friend except Dr. Stark."

Drosée turned her softly shadowed blue eyes inquiringly on her impetuous friend. Dr. Stark had seated himself at her right, and Jo was on the piano-stool near; Mrs. Fielding sat opposite the three, looking a little flushed, and remarkably handsome. Her usually nonchalant air, and the calmness of her brown eyes, were gone. She was in earnest now.

"Fairvalley is inexpressibly petty and pretentious, as you know. You have always attracted the greatest notice here. Whenever you two girls have gone out, you have received attention enough to make you the belles of such society as 'tis. But I made the mistake, and we all made the mistake, of being rather exclusive; you, Dr. Stark, and you, Drosée and Jo, and Wilmer and I, were very happy together, and we all refused some invitations, and neglected some social duties in order to enjoy our club. We were talked about, and it got out that we were all of us free-thinkers, and the like—which is abominable nonsense, though all of us haven't the same ideas of religious duty"—with a shy smile towards Dr. Stark. "Then, my dear Drosée, I must confess I fear Mr. Bell was illiberal enough to say some spiteful things about you, as a member of the other church—the man hates Dr. Bampfyle, and everything about him. And *then* you made powerful enemies in your own church—and you know society in Fairvalley is churchly, or it is nothing."

"You remember that I warned you against this Mrs. Estwick?" said Dr. Stark, quietly. "I saw how the wind blew at that party at her mother's in July.

She had brought out that blue-stocking heiress simply to outdo you if possible; and your innocent enjoyment at that party, and the way that old Wilmer, whom she had specially destined for the heiress, dangled after you, was gall to her vinegar. And then when her own husband went over to you, and you snubbed him so deliciously to her very face——"

"But, Dr. Stark, I do not remember a word of all that," said Drosée, quite seriously. "Her husband is quite an old man—as old as my father—and I only talked to him a short time—and since then I have met him, and he has been very polite, and just as friendly and courteous as can be."

"No doubt that he still admires you, child," said Mrs. Fielding, quickly. "Indeed, I have heard him defend you publicly when Mrs. Estwick made some sharp speech about you—but that did you no good, in any way."

Dr. Stark had risen restlessly, and begun to pace the floor.

"It is just this," he said turning, as Mrs. Fielding ceased; "Mr. Estwick is an old man, and you are a beautiful, innocent young woman. You have never done or said a single wrong thing since you came to this miserable little town. But Mrs. Estwick is a coarse, jealous creature, and her husband has sometimes justified her jealousy by his elderly gallantries. And all the harm one venomous tongue can do, will be done you here. That is the whole story, and I wish to heaven you need never hear a word of it. But it is necessary, if you intend to live here. Avoid all that set. Understand that you—even you!—have enemies; and—*feel* that you have friends!"

He paused just an instant before her, and then walked on again, and stood looking out of the window.

"What do people *say?*" asked Drosée, after a little pause.

"Since your novel came out, they say that you are— oh! a thousand things," said Mrs. Fielding, impatiently. "Some of them admire it; most of them don't understand it; and the most definite as well as the most absurd charge I have heard against you is that 'the chief singer in Trinity choir is an atheist.' I think our people have the credit of originating that racy rumor."

Drosée had started to her feet. A stern, indignant light shone in her beautiful eyes, and her lips were

shaped into an expression of dumb protest. Mrs.
Fielding caught her hands, and Jo exclaimed:

"It is the kind of thing she might expect! They
dare not utter a syllable against her as a woman, and
so they accuse her as a thinker! And this is what
comes of envy and senseless jealously, is it? Drosée,
if I were you, I would shake the dust of Fairvalley
off my feet, and turn my back on it for ever and
ever!"

"I suppose," said Drosée with a faint sigh, sitting
down again, "that this 'all comes in the day's work'?
I never had such an experience as this before. It will
be valuable to me as an experience, perhaps! It shows
me how slight a motive can in real life make a woman
malevolent and ready to injure a girl who never consciously offended her. It is not worth while to regret
it, I suppose. It is a fact, and I must face it."

Dr. Stark came back from the window, gravely
took up Drosée's hand, pressed it, relinquished it, and
sat down again at her side.

"I am going, Drosée," said Mrs. Fielding, rising.
with a mist coming over her brown eyes. "Oh, my
little philosopher," she whispered, as she kissed her,

"your spirit is fate's recompense to you for all your ills."

Drosée kissed her, and went with her to the door.

"Good-bye, Jo," said Mrs. Fielding. "Good evening, Dr. Stark. No, Drosée, do not come out with me. Good-bye to you all—I shall see you out at home soon, I hope;" and so saying, she was gone.

"You have been traveling, and you are tired, I fear," said Dr. Stark, turning back into the parlor, nevertheless. "But it is a great pleasure to see her back again, isn't it, Miss Josephus?"

"Sit down, Dr. Stark," said Jo. "Drosée never was so tired in her life that she wasn't glad to see you. You must take tea with us to-night. I am going to have a place put for you, and make your favorite muffins—so make yourself at home, like a good boy." And Jo, with a glimpse of her native gayety, appropriated Dr. Stark's umbrella and hat, and walked away with them.

Those who only knew Dr. Stark as a politician and a trenchant and sarcastic reviewer, would have been amazed to see these two young women so familiar with him; but bitter and terrible as this stooping, plain little man could be to those he disliked or despised, he was another creature here.

He sat down by Drosée, and said, with a gentle sigh :

"And so our club is dispersed and scattered abroad. Mrs. Fielding and Miss Jo go next week, and you and Wilmer broke the charm six weeks ago."

"Where is Mr. Wilmer, and how is he?" asked Drosée, quietly, but not without a slight change of countenance as she put the question.

"He is in New York, pegging away at his law books, and going unshaved," said Dr. Stark, with a shrewd but smiling eye. "I think the lad is in love, and I suspect that it is going rather hard with him; but he's such a proud, shy young Lucifer, that I try to pretend I don't see it." Drosée's color deepened, and Dr. Stark changed the subject lightly. "He gave me a rough copy of some verses the other day—not a love poem—some nonsense about an inebriated frog. He says he wrote them when a temperance meeting was held here in Fairvalley last June. Would you like to have a laugh over them?"

"Yes," said Drosée, simply. " You have them with you ?"

"I think so," said Dr. Stark, pulling from his breast pocket a handful of letters and papers, and shuffling them like a pack of cards. "Yes, here it is—if you want to see what fantastic ideas can come into a wise man's head. That lad is as full of humors and conceits and as variable as the wind in spring. Now here he goes—" ' A dozen verses on an inebriated frog.' (Heaven knows how such an idea occurred to him—cold water drinkers, I always thought—but it must have made this fellow a more glaring instance of frailty.)"

Drosée, laughing, held out her hand for the paper. Dr. Stark gave it her. It was a scrap of tumbled "legal cap," written in a small, decided, orderly hand, with a hard lead pencil—nothing remarkable about it. But there shot a strange thrill through every sensitive fiber of Drosée's frame, as her fingers touched this bit of Wilmer's writing; and the whimsical lines were folded up, quietly appropriated, and treasured by her afterwards as if they had been the choicest specimen of amatory verse.

As she folded the paper with an assumed air of

absent-mindedness, Dr. Stark carelessly replaced his letters in his pocket, and went on to say :

"That poem of yours in your novel was a fine one, Drosée. I am proud of your book, child, and Wilmer admires it vastly."

"Does he?" said Drosée, the rich color leaping instantly to her pale cheeks, and then fading swiftly.

"But you will do better yet," went on this Mentor, earnestly. " Your promise is beyond your performance as yet."

" That is the kindest thing you can say !" she returned gratefully.

" You give a prominence in this story to one passion that you must learn to estimate more truly," Dr. Stark went on. "Love is not all of life, you know, nor even most of it, to the majority of us. It has its place in life ; but it is neither the greatest good nor chiefest misery of a noble life."

Drosée sat with her hands clasped in her lap, looking seriously and fixedly at one spot in the carpet.

"It is the best thing, but not the only thing," she said quietly. " And," smiling, " it proves a fine discipline for some natures. I think I used it in that way, in the book."

Dr. Stark shook his head.

"Lovers may think that part of it very true and sweet," he said. "But you made a mistake. Great miseries rise from profounder depths than conjugal relations. True, an old poet says :

> "'Those we love best have most the power to harm us :
> We lay our sleeping lives within their arms'

—but it is a *young* character who says it. When older, we find these but bodkin scratches compared to those we get from other quarters, when the professional torturers of the universe take rope and wheel in hand and begin operations."

Drosée lifted her eyes suddenly and looked at her friend. The bitter accents of his tongue were not matched by any expression in his face. He looked as calm and phlegmatic as he ever did.

"There is little in life which has any other than a comparative value," said Drosee, thoughtfully. "The best of everything is in being, not in having, good."

"You are learning the art of life," said Mentor,

gravely. "Indeed, this life does seem to me inexpressibly petty and insignificant in all its activities."

"And yet—!" cried Drosée, and stopped, with a sudden sigh. She was trying to grow quiet, to desire, to strive for nothing; this very day she had taken a lesson in indifference to the world; but the direct utterance of a sentiment so unlike Wilmer's, who was full of fine and hopeful ideas as to a definite aim in life, gave her a momentary shock. Her theories might accord more with those of the elder man, but her heart went with the younger.

"Life is the instrument by which we are rounded and molded," Drosée went on, more quietly. "Acts and emotions all come into play in that, and go to shape—or break—us. There is some reason for every turn, and some object for the result."

"Our life has some reason—some object? Proof on that point would be acceptable—but grant it; has it any reason or object *for us?*"

"Its reason and object is to form in us that temper and spirit towards God which shall be worthy of life hereafter," said Drosée, boldly.

" Pish !" said Dr. Stark, turning aside. But Drosée went on :

" There isn't anything of some people *to* live. Take away their little vanities and harsh habits of mind and worldly interest, and there isn't the ghost of an individuality left. The immortal part of us is love of truth and right and goodness. 'Nothing can be everlasting, nothing in the universe of God lasts forever, but holiness.' "

" Is *that* your theory as to the immortality of the soul ?" said Dr. Stark abruptly, as she ceased. Jo had come in quietly during the last minute, and now sat looking from one to the other with attentive and thoughtful eyes. There was no trace of the dimpling and childish expression in her serious face. Jo was a woman now, and no ordinary one.

" I believe," said Drosée, without hesitation, " that ' the wages of sin is death '—absolute death ; and that ' eternal life is the gift of God through Jesus Christ our Lord.' That is my belief—and Jo's "—with a glance at her younger sister, whose soft hand was now thrust into hers.

Dr. Stark smiled, and took a turn down the room.

"The soul is immortal, child," he said, grimly. "As to personal immortality no man can tell. But that the life once given can ever be withdrawn no reasoning can successfully maintain. I know there have been instances of your way of thinking from the times of the 'early fathers' of your church down to these. I cannot myself see that your notion is alien to the spirit of Christianity. But it is too much and too little to believe."

"You are a pagan, Dr. Stark," said Drosée, but with mildness. She had risen, and taken a small book from the shelves, and now began to read aloud: " 'The prevailing doctrine respecting our immortality is, and has for the most part been, that the soul is naturally and essentially immortal; that the life imparted to it at its creation is a thing that having once been, must forever be; that it is dependent on nothing outside of itself for sustenance and support, but is in such a sense self-supporting that no withdrawal of the favor or the support of its Creator on the one hand, nor any inflictions of his wrath on the other, can in the least affect the strength of its hold upon life, or the conditions upon which the perpetuity of its existence depend; in spite of itself, and in spite of all assaults of finite evil, and all withdrawal of divine support, living by the inherent necessity of its own nature. This is not only the pagan doctrine, but, strange to say, the prevalent Christian doctrine, notwithstanding that it finds no support in scripture, and is contrary to reason, and to the analogy of nature and Christianity.' "

"That will do!—What book is that?"

"'The Philosophy of the Trinitarian Doctrine,' by the Rev. A. G. Pease. I wish you would read it."

"I will, if you desire it, but it is not likely to impress me much," said Dr. Stark, smiling. "No, Drosée. The soul lives because it comes from a living God, and exists while he exists. It cannot be dissociated from him, and therefore it is held in life. For in words which I profoundly believe, 'in him we live, and move, and have our being.' We are part of him, or we are nothing: we are already in eternity; we cannot escape from it."

"I see what you mean," said Jo, suddenly. "It agrees with this book. Drosée, give it to me. May I read this?"

"I listen," said Dr. Stark, courteously.

Jo began.

"'All life is organic , ... beneath the throne of God there is not such a thing as life that does not belong to a living species. And moreover, there is no such thing as a species that does not constitute an organic unity, consisting of its fountain-head and members.'"

Dr. Stark nodded.

"You are quick and right, Miss Jo. How does your author dispose of his own admission, though?"

"'It is impossible,'" went on Jo, "'that there should be any such thing as life in an individual which he does not derive from the life-principle or fountain-head to which he belongs . . . The life of the body implies the life of the members. The member that is separated from the body instantly dies . . . The soul has no alternative. It must maintain its normal relations with the life of God, or it must perish. For God so loved the world that he gave his only begotten Son, that whosoever believeth in him should not perish, but have everlasting life!'"

"Some of that is good so far as it goes," said Dr.

Stark. "But what is strong enough to sever the relation of my soul to God's?"

"Willful sin," said this youngest theologian, softly. "'Sin, when it is finished, bringeth forth death.'"

"I see that you two girls have considered your theory and studied it," said Dr. Stark quietly. "It is an unusual thing for two young creatures like you to think so much on these themes. You, Jo, I had always believed orthodox."

"I am," said Jo, serenely. "The church is large enough to include all shades of belief. While I say the Creed, and believe it, I am an orthodox churchwoman. There are many who believe as we do, though they will not say so; and many who would so believe, if they were not in the habit of thoughtlessly accepting current doctrines, and content in believing that the hereafter will instruct them, and that there is no use in bothering about minor beliefs nowadays."

Dr. Stark could not help smiling: Jo's dry way was inimitable.

"And are you two agreed, then?" he said, turning to Drosée.

"So far," said Drosée, in a low voice. Then she

added, more clearly; "the one thing *I* have not yet felt my mind settled about, is whether *personal* immortality is to be won."

"Ah! there we meet again," said the Doctor. "It may be a weakness, but I ardently long for personal immortality. I have slight interest in this world, and care not a jot what succeeds me; I have no longing for posthumous fame, or any such 'lease of immortality;' mankind may forget me, or set me down either as fathomless fool, or arrant knave; and if I consciously exist, I shall either not know it, or not care for it; but yet this desire to live clings to me; and though I see no proof that I shall, still I want to preserve my individual life in the world to come."

"How strange!" said Drosée, softly. "I do not think that I care. To return to God as 'a flask of water broken into the sea' is all I desire. I want to live with a will in unison with his; and when I die I am willing that his will be done. I wish nothing beyond. 'Emptied, and lost, and swallowed up in thee'—that is enough. So I do not trouble myself to question anything except that I am continually his."

There was a perfect, unaffected simplicity in these

gently-uttered words. It was a confession uttered in the manner of an opinion—slowly and thoughtfully. Dr. Stark looked intently at her fair, unconscious face.

"Your mind is a philosopher's, but your temperament is that of a quietist," he said. "Had you been born a few centuries back, and a man, you would have founded a new order of monks, Drosée, or written some great mystical religious work."

"How strangely you think!" said Drosée, looking at him attentively.

"But, Drosée, it is not right!" said Jo, quickly. "Personal immortality is just what Christ teaches, and promises to believers. Don't you remember? 'This day *thou* shalt be with me in Paradise.' "

"Yes—that seems very clear," said Drosée, musingly.

"So you desire and expect personal immortality, uniting our differences?" said Dr. Stark, turning to Jo.

Jo answered gravely.

" 'Not as though I had already attained '—but 'if by any means I might attain to the resurrection of the dead.' "

—This was the last of that grave talk. A diversion

9*

was created by Mr. Alwyn's entrance, and the bells ringing for supper; and the rest of the evening was passed in light converse, which touched upon nothing that nearly concerned the speakers.

CHAPTER VIII.

"I pray the prayer of Plato old:
　　God make thee beautiful within,
And let thine eyes the good behold,
　　In everything save sin!"—J. G. WHITTIER.

"Love, that what time his own hands guard his head
　The whole world's wrath and strength shall not strike dead;
Love, that if once his own hands make his grave
The whole world's pity and sorrow shall not save."
　　　　　　　　　　—A. C. SWINBURNE.

LEFT quite alone by the departure of Jo and of
Mrs. Fielding, Drosée was without any near friend of
her own sex. Jo had gone away so soon after ac-
quainting Drosée with her intentions that no line was
written to the Seafords of her plans until they were
already carried into effect. No explanation as to Jo's
unlucky love was ever even begun; Jo was too proud
and Drosée too forbearing for the subject ever to be
mentioned. General conversation on theories and
books, special discussions of the work their hands were

busy with, and talk of Fairvalley and its ways sufficiently occupied their tongues. Jo's one expressed regret at leaving home was that she couldn't stay to fight the neighborhood for Drosée!

"I will have it out of some of these old women, yet," she stoutly declared. "Something or other will make them sorry, yet. There are more ways of killing a horse than standing him on his head in a mill-pond."

Drosée could only laugh at this impromptu proverb.

"I would give up going, for your sake, if I could," Jo went on, ruefully.

"But you cannot, and we won't think of it," Drosee answered, cheerfully. "It is all for the best, as it is. But isn't it a wonder that father acquiesced with such meekness? He hasn't been like himself of late."

"He could be introduced to himself as a new character," Jo said, "he is so mild and sunny. Prosperity is good for him, I think—poor old Pater! The money he got for that play agrees with him wonderfully."

And so Jo—cheery, saucy Jo, with brave eyes and dimpled cheeks, after a laughing struggle in the embraces of Jemima, and one kiss delivered to the Pater, and one extra kiss to Drosée, and a faint clinging to her sister's hand—was gone from Fairvalley. In two more days Fanny Fielding went, and Drosée was left to her. self.

The company that offered itself to her was that of men, it appeared. Fairvalley swains—noticeably young Thorndike, just home from Europe, and Keene, a rising lawyer in the little town—were as devoted to her about this time as she would permit; Dolton, the tenor in the choir, scarcely knew which he was most enamored of, the deep-set, big bright eyes, the fine flickering red of her fair cheek, or the heavenly voice that bore his own along with mellow, measured notes when they sang their famous duet in the Te Deum, the Sunday the bishop was there. These men Drosée treated politely, and gave to them what pleasure she found herself rightly able to give; but they dropped away again before long, at least to all appearance; they found her "different from other people;" they were not at home with her, finding her insensible to flattery, unfavorable to gossip, and able to critically and logically dispute any pretentious assumptions of knowledge and superiority. A candid, simple, intelligent mind, not at all assuming the attitude of a distinctly feminine one, and a manner whose subtile aloofness could never be forgotten, was not the thing to attract men like these permanently. "Kings cannot force the exquisite reserve of distance." Miss Alwyn was distant, and her admirers were obliged to yield her up.

Dr. Bampfyle called upon this parishioner of his twice about this time. Mrs. Estwick saw him go in the first time, and Mrs. Howard met him as he came out the second time; but when these ladies attempted to fathom the reason of his visits—for this rather ascetic divine called rarely on any one, and almost never on the young ladies of his church, though making himself readily approachable to the young men of it—he gave very scant satisfaction to them. It was impossible to associate the name of this revered and lofty preacher with any pretty woman's, merely because he visited her; but though these visits were, in fact, those of a pastor, and the conversation on such themes as a thoughtful and religious teacher might think it wise to suggest to an earnest listener, they did not escape attention, and when by chance these two happened to walk two blocks together down the street one afternoon,

Mrs. Estwick did think that Miss Alwyn's forwardness was becoming town-talk!

Nor were the gossips better pleased that Drosée's most constant companion was the bowed and brown little man they all half admired and half disliked. Nothing she did pleased the cavilers, and when Jo had been gone six weeks Drosée woke up to the fact that there was not a lady in Fairvalley to whom she owed a visit, or from whom she had had any recent kindly greeting. Mrs. Burbage, Mr. Keene's sister, had "cut" her on the street soon after she had declined some of Mr. Keene's attentions; and Mrs. Gage, Mrs. Estwick's cousin, had omitted her name altogether from her invitations to a rather large and church-y party. She was in nobody's circle; that was evident at last.

Drosée realized that her popularity was gone. Perhaps not irretrievably, if she chose to make an effort to re-establish it. She questioned herself to see if there was any bitterness in this loss of popular admiration, or anything to be gained by winning it back. She knew something of the world, and her own power to please when she exerted herself. She knew that, with due attention, a sufficient expenditure of time, a little of what is called "diplomacy," and her native quickness, tact, and address, she could take a sufficiently prominent place in Fairvalley society to dazzle some, and to mortify those she could not win. She had tested her skill and power in former days, and been a belle before she was a philosopher.

Surely, much had already been attained by a young and fair woman, who had learned not to disquiet herself in vain over trifles, and to renounce selfish desires of love, and all care for pretentious ways of living; who had put aside pride, and love of fame, and heeded not clamor and evil speaking; but admiration in some form is dear to nearly every heart. How much was it worth to Drosée?

She considered, and renounced all effort for it. "I desire nothing that popularity can give me, or revenge afford me, or display supply," she determined. The good of a quiet life she was ready to perceive. She thought, studied, wrote in peace; she helped Jemima, corresponded with Jo, attended to her father's various requirements, and brightened the dull November evenings to the one friend she saw frequently—the bitter, faithful, eccentric, thoughtful little man who stood by her, Dr. Stark.

And just then, in the brown falling of the leaves, came a sudden whirlwind of angry passion to test and try the composure our philosopher was set to attain.

Mrs. Johns, her old friend, had been away for some time, but had now returned to Fairvalley, rented a furnished villa from a family gone to New York for the season, and decided to take up her residence here for the winter. She and her kindly old husband came driving by one day and called for Drosée to go out with them in their carriage; as it happened, she was obliged to decline; and the next evening she went up to see the good lady in her new quarters.

Miss Ball happened to open the door. She blushed in her usual juvenile and embarrassed manner when she saw Drosée, and following her into the bright sitting-room where Mrs. Johns sat, took away her work-basket and pile of sewing with great haste, and disappeared.

"Jane!" called Mrs. Johns, having welcomed Drosée with effusion—"excuse me a minute, dear—Jane,"

following her, " companion " into the hall, and whispering, " don't *she* know yet ?"

" No, no, Cousin Mercy," said Jane, redder than
any peony, " and *don't* let it out !   *He'll* tell her soon."

" Well, it's your affair, child, but I *would* tell her
before it gets out," said the old lady, beaming through
her glasses at the " child " of five-and-thirty; and so
went back to the sitting-room.

But it came to pass that Mrs. Johns *did* " let it
out," under a most unexpected shock. She had been
making much of Drosée, taking her about the lower
floor of her house to show her all her convenient and
pretty arrangements—for the old lady was very fond
of housekeeping, and glad that her wandering and half
invalid husband had been willing to settle down to it
for a while; she had made Drosée eat a bit of cake,
and offered her wine, lemonade, and jelly, in turn, only
half satisfied to pour out ice-water at last into a goblet
almost as thin and light as a bubble; and then, when
they had come back and taken a seat by the deep window in the sitting-room, where a flourishing hanging-
basket was over-running with vines, Mrs. Johns made
some allusion to Drosée's successful novel.

"Don't, please!" Drosée said, with a half-comic, half-candid air of entreaty. "So many severe things have been said about my simple little book that I shiver at its name."

"I thought it was mighty pretty," Mrs. Johns said, stoutly. "I cried over it, and I laughed over it. It's a wonderful book, my dear. *I* liked it better'n any of your father's books," in a deprecatory undertone. She thought that this was, perhaps, too unjustifiable, for of course the elder member of the family knew more about writing than the younger, so she hurried on. "And I heard lots of people speak about it when I was away."

"Dear Mrs. Johns, it is very kind of you to tell me this, and you don't know how pleasant it is to have you like it," Drosée replied, gratefully.

"I can't say I understood all of it, my dear. And it might seem wrong in you, to some who didn't know you, to let some of the people go wrong, and some of 'em talk as if a pagan religion was as good as their own; but people *are* cranky and sinful, and I know it ain't you that's to blame."

"Thank you," Drosée said, smiling. "There is a great deal that is beautiful and like our religion in those which people used to ignorantly call idolatrous; and one ought to be glad of all the beauty and truth time discovers to us, don't you think?"

"Y—yes, certainly," Mrs. Johns assented, very *uncertainly*. "I wouldn't meddle with those things much, though, my dear; if they agree with the Bible, they don't teach nothing new; and if they don't, they are not safe handling."

"Why, Mrs. Johns, you are like the Caliph Omar," Drosée exclaimed, laughing. "That was just his idea, so he had a great many valuable books burned, because if they didn't agree with the Koran they were untrue, and if they did they were unnecessary."

"Now, Drosée, what heathenish books you must have been reading! What have you to do in a Christian country with Caliphs and Korans? Do, my dear, let these outlandish things alone, and it will be all the better for you."

Drosée smiled gently, and hesitated to answer; then she said, impulsively:

" All truth must agree with truth, you see; and I believe the Bible is true, and can stand the severest tests; but surely God is not revealed in that alone. Don't you know a great man has said, 'God has written the Gospel not only in the Bible, but in trees and flowers, stars and clouds;' and so——"

"I can't argue with you, dear; that sounds very pretty, but the man who said that——"

"It was Martin Luther, Mrs. Johns!" Drosée interpolated, before the good lady should commit herself.

"Martin Luther—the Reformer?" Mrs. Johns asked, slightly staggered. "Well, he was a good and wise man, no doubt, but I'm no believer in men's wisdom, and no great of a churchwoman, neither; the Bible is my foundation, and there I take my stand!"

The beaming, lovely old face was quite flushed with excitement. Drosée saw that it had been a mistake to discuss any religious topic with this old friend of hers; she did not understand a word Drosée had said, and had only a vague idea that somehow she was not agreed with.

"I hope you do not think that I am sorry to have you stand there," Drosée said, in a deprecatory way. "I care for our own Scriptures and our own beliefs as warmly as possible. I am only glad that other people in other times worshipped this same Creator, and I revere every pure desire of him expressed in *any* religion."

Mrs. Johns looked at the young face before her with a dubious expression, an instant, and then melted.

"You poor, dear child! Drosée, I loved you long before I knew whose child you were, and I ain't stopped since I knew you was Emily Windham's. I can trust her blood, for you're both of you honest through and through. We won't argufy, dear; I'll pray for you, Drosée, and the Lord 'll lead you safe, I know."

"Oh, Mrs. Johns," Drosée exclaimed, resting her head upon the wide breast to which she had been suddenly caught in a fond embrace, "I do so want to hear you tell about my mother! I have often wished I could make up my mind to ask you about her, but I have not talked of her for so long. I shall never cease to regret her; I shall never cease to want the mother-love I have lacked so long; I always think that *she* would have understood perfectly!"

"Poor child! You must learn to think of her in heaven——"

"Heaven! *Dead?*" Drosée cried, lifting a horror-stricken face. "Oh, I have always hoped that somehow, yet—that while she was living, somewhere, it was yet possible——"

"Living!" Mrs. Johns exclaimed, more bewildered than Drosée. "Ain't she been dead all these years? Ain't your father a widower? Ain't he engaged this minute to Jane Ball?"

"Father? My father?" Drosée said, with suppressed vehemence of speech, as she rose to her feet. "Would any woman wish to marry my father, who nearly broke the truest heart that ever beat?"

"Where is he? Where is Jane Ball?" Mrs. Johns exclaimed, excitedly. "What does he mean by it? Oh, child, you have given me such a start!" And Mrs. Johns sunk back in attempting to rise, and fainted quietly.

Drosée bent over her helplessly an instant, then fanned her, rubbed her hands, and attempted to loosen her dress, but finding herself unequal to this, and the swoon a serious one, summoned help. In a moment a servant, followed by Miss Ball, had come to her assistance, and the three removed Mrs. Johns to the sofa, and began to apply the usual restoratives.

"What on earth has done it? She hasn't fainted before in five months; I thought she was quite over these attacks," said poor Miss Jane, busily unfastening the rather tight dark silk. "Isn't it strange, well as she looks—she weighs a hundred and seventy-five if it's a pound! Oh! Cousin Mercy! Ah, you're better—that's nicely, now—no, keep still—just smell this, dear!" And Miss Jane's crimson face lit up with relief and joy as Mrs. Johns opened her eyes and feebly moved her hand.

"Let me sit up," Mrs. Johns said, presently. "No, Susan, you can go. Don't you go scare Mr. Johns telling him when he comes in. Jane, get me a glass of cordial, please. Thank you, dear," to Drosée, who remained fanning her.

"I want you to tell Jane," she continued, as soon as the others were out of hearing. "It's a dreadful thing, but it must be done, and done now."

"No, Mrs. Johns," Drosée answered, decidedly; "it is not my business to offer any information to Miss Ball. My father is the one to tell her. And perhaps she knows more than you think. My father's divorce is perhaps such that he can legally marry. I will see him, not her. Rest a little, and do not worry now."

"Divorce or no divorce—oh! poor Emily!—if he's got a wife living he won't have Jane for another with *my* consent," said Mrs. Johns, with surprising vigor. "It ain't Scripture, it ain't decency, it ain't——"

"Do not talk now, Cousin Mercy," said Jane Ball's voice in unusually firm accents. She had come in with the cordial. She was deeply flushed, as always by excitement, but her big blue eyes were brave and even defiant. "Drink your cordial, cousin."

"Jane, did you know it?" asked Mrs. Johns, in the tone of one deeply hurt and wronged.

"Your father," said Miss Ball, addressing herself to Drosée and not to Mrs. Johns, "has told me his whole past. I have accepted it. I alone understand him as no one else does. This is between him and me. You had no right to trouble my cousin so."

"It was surprised out of her," Mrs. Johns replied

for Drosee, "and out of me, Jane, she added, with a sudden sense of having betrayed confidence.

"Miss Alwyn," said Miss Ball, her eyes filling with sudden tears, and her richly-colored, juvenile face looking even younger in its pathos, " I love your father, I admire him, I will be a good wife to him and brighten his life ; can't we be friends?" She held out her large, full hand cordially.   A pang went through Drosée's heart as she withheld her own.

" As his—wife, I could never recognize you, Miss Ball," she said, in an agitated tone. "As a woman, you compel me to respect your loyalty ; but you do not know my father ; and I am sorry, deeply sorry, for the injury he has done you."

" I know your father, and I know that he has been hardly and unjustly treated even by his own family, and ill-used by a cruel fate," Miss Ball said, unconsciously echoing her elderly lover's own words to her. " Your mother—your mother was so wicked and harsh as to be unworthy the name of woman !"

With those words the usually serene face of Drosée was transformed ; a furious and terrible rage shot from her deep blue eyes, and her very lips turned pale with passion. The last effort of her self-control closed them, and she turned aside, walked across the room rapidly, though trembling at every step, opened the door, and perfectly heedless of Mrs. Johns' exclamations and Miss Ball's hesitating "Miss Drosée!" she passed out of the house, through the gate, and found herself in the shady road leading homewards. She passed along it, conquering her trembling in the bracing air, but still pale and torn with passion, which she still repressed. At the second crossing she paused; she felt her emotion capable of wildly asserting itself at sight of any familiar face. To see her father now would be unbearable; even good old Jemima's face would be an intolerable weight on the scale against self-mastery. She turned aside, and walked blindly, swiftly, and as if instinctively, toward the strange and straggling end of town, and into the open country.

It was not until she stood on the brow of the first hill rising beyond Fairvalley that Drosée knew that she had been walking toward that old homestead of her mother's family that her father had pointed out to her on that drive with Mrs. Johns last summer. In her present mood, that spot was irresistibly attractive to her; she turned her face thitherward, and more calmly continued her walk in that direction.

As she went, her mind became clearer, and the reflected over the discovery of the afternoon, and decided on her best course of action—an appeal to the influence of her father's wealthy and only sister, Mrs. Seaford, to whom he was deeply in debt—in case it proved that he was really legally free to marry and determined to do so. In case he ultimately did so, and even under the present circumstances of his intention, the matter of feeling was more difficult to decide than that of action. The intensest wrath and scorn rose again and again within her, and that difficult lesson of tranquillity seemed harder than ever before to learn. Will, pride, and anger—they are hard to reason into just moderation. Drosée walked on, with fierce and dark companions. It seemed to her that she could *never* submit to this injustice and wrong with quietness, that it must forever embitter her if defeated in her will to restrain this open wickedness. No one had ever seen Drosée as she looked on this afternoon, when she walked away from Fairvalley; it was not the philosopher Mrs. Fielding talked of who went with flame-lit cheek and sternly-blazing deep blue eyes, through wayside dust and falling leaves unheeding.

At a distance of more than two miles from Fair-valley Drosée paused, having reached the low stone fence bounding the little farm; fatigued, she went close to it, and leaning against a tree, looked wistfully over it into the shady orchard beyond, with its long, rank, neglected grass. She could just see a corner of the low, old-fashioned house through the trees. She wanted to go nearer. The place was silent and deserted. She climbed the broad, low stone fence with ease, and jumped down into the long grass of the orchard. Walking up through the trees she soon came within sight of the house. She seemed to remember the place as if she had known it in some former existence, but, to her keen disappointment, it appeared that the house was inhabited, after all. A feather-bed hung out in the sun from an upper window. A red rocking-chair was visible at a lower window, and a light table near it was piled with books. A cat was dozing in the sunshine on the porch. Everything was quiet, but orderly; the flower-beds were weeded, and some autumn flowers yet bloomed there; the broad stone before the doorsteps was clean, the path freshly graveled.

Drosée turned back. The old house was not going to ruin, then. She must not even pluck one of the red rose-haws on that clambering vine. She could not go around the corner to that old-fashioned well with its long pole, and drink, as somehow she found she had meant to drink, a draught of water from its cool depths. When Drosée was a tiny girl, her mother had taught her the verses about the "Old Oaken Bucket," and told her about the well in the yard at home, and all the poetry of that familiarly-quoted old ballad had been associated in her mind with her memories of her mother's stories of a happy childhood. Drosée knew that two bright, deep eyes, like her own, had peeped over the boards and looked eagerly down into the mysterious depths of water and bit of sky so far, far down below.

She went along through the orchard, and came out on a grove of young trees sloping down into a small natural glen in whose depths sparkled water. Drosée went down the stony declivity to the brook, which purled between fern-banks. The leaves of the oaks and beeches waved above her in the light afternoon breeze. Birds flew through the tree-tops. The world seemed leagues away. Drosée sat down on the grass, leaned back against a large, smoothly-shelving rock, turned, put her cheek against its coolness, and closed her eyes. The shadows kept guard over her; the brook and the birds sang to her; peace stole in through every sense. Drosée gave herself up to the reactionary quiet, and with a sigh which did not all belong to sorrow, she gave herself up to wandering and peaceful thoughts, remote from recent trouble. She was trying to remember herself and Jo as children; trying to recall the face of the mother she had not seen since her twelfth year; smiling at sudden recollections of old frolics with Louis, and softening under the remembrance of the faithful motherly nursing which had guarded her in her most serious childish illnesses.

Whether these thoughts had glided into dreams Drosée could not tell, but suddenly she started, and if she had been asleep was awakened. A tall woman dressed in black, with a fair but stern countenance, and dark, familiar eyes, was looking down at her from the other side of the glen.   Drosée moved and rose slowly; her eyes, and the deep, unforgotten eyes now regarding her, held each other in one unbroken gaze; and both women moved silently down the glen, towards the narrow brook; Drosée reached it first, unconsciously, and her feet were in the clear, shallow water before she was aware of it.

"Child! child!" exclaimed the other, in a strange, tender, chiding voice : and then Drosée knew certainly who spoke to her.

"Mother!" she cried; and leaping to the opposite shore, she was clasped in a trembling, straining embrace, and held her mother to her with a fervent, passionate strength.   Their cheeks were together—the mother's cold and wan, the daughter's soft and hot; they moved only to look into each other's faces : and then Drosée saw that the firm lines about her mother's face were melted, her lips tremulous, and her eyelids red.

"Mother!   My darling mother!" Drosée said, in a voice of such soft and caressing enthusiasm that it was more like a lover's than a child's : and then the two kissed each other with a kind of awed delight in their new-found joy.

"My daughter!" the mother said, placing her arm in Drosée's, to turn and walk with her up the glen. "You are a woman!" she said, pausing. "A good girl, my child?" passing her hand lovingly over Drosée's forehead and cheek, and then looking with a fond anxiety into the fair face. The question carried Drosée back more than ten years, on the instant. She remembered the words, the tone, the look; the confessional at her mother's knee every night, and the advice and the prayers that came after it, and all the careful, anxious, but ever-loving mother-ways. She answered now only by a confiding look; and the two went up the hill together.

"Mother, who lives here now?" she asked, as they came within sight of the old house again.

"I live here, my child. The cousin who bought it left it to me in his will. All this is mine again. I have come here to make it my home."

"And you—we have been living so near you! All of us in this one little town of Fairvalley! Did you know——"

10*

"Yes, I knew. I meant to have seen you soon. But my dépôt, and church, and post-office, are at Brakesburg, which lies in that direction," pointing eastward. "I have only been here a little while. Is my other child well, Drosée? Is little Jo well—and grown, too?"

"Grown and well, dear mother. It has been so many years since you saw us, hasn't it? I was twelve——"

"Twice since then I have seen you," the mother said. "Once in church—I came to New York to get that glimpse of you—and once at West Point; you were there with your aunt, I suppose; I went over for a day with some of the girls of the school. That was long ago. I have been abroad five years."

"Why didn't you speak to us, mother? Where have you been, darling? Talk to me—talk fast!"

The grave face smiled and then saddened again.

"I was bound never to seek you out or address you willfully," she said. "I know now how foolish I was ever to agree to that. I have suffered for it. Drosée, is your father kind to you? Do you girls love him? Is—is he well?"

"He is well," Drosée said, gravely. "He is usually as kind as—as it is his nature to be."

There was a pause. "You have been abroad?" Drosée asked.

"For several years I was teaching, in two different large schools; then I went with Georgine Palliser and her mother, to Europe. Mrs. Palliser needed me and I could not refuse. She was one of my truest and oldest friends: but you can't remember her, I suppose."

"I remember the name. Go on, dear mother!"

"We educated Georgine abroad. She was married last spring, at Florence, to a Boston gentleman,—a Mr. Vincent. Mrs. Palliser died in Paris in June, and I came home with the Vincents. I have been with them until now. This property was bequeathed me last summer by my cousin, and with what I have been able to lay up, I am able now to rest and call my children to me. I am in feeble health, and I must have my children! I have been very weak. If I had not been so cowardly, I might have found some way to keep you with me all this time, rearing you as a mother should. But I will do what I can even now."

They passed within the low doorway, and up the crooked stairs.

It was growing dark before Drosée's brook-wet feet had been rubbed and warmed to her mother's satisfaction, and re-clad in dry stockings and a pair of slim slippers which were furnished her. The mother's solicitous promptness in attending personally to this matter brought both tears and smiles to Drosée's face; she, who had felt herself a woman of much independence heretofore, enjoyed the novelty of being watched and cared for like a child. This over, the mother led the daughter again down-stairs, into her low dining-room, where a table was spread with supper for two.

"You are my guest to-night, Drosée," the mother said; and leaving her standing by a chair passed to her own accustomed seat, and bending a grave face as she stood with her hand on the back of her chair, she briefly uttered a petition for blessing before seating herself.

A small hickory-wood fire snapped and blazed in the great fireplace behind a polished brass fender; the table was set with a simple supper, and its arrange-ments were tasteful and refined. The glass and spoons and two pieces of old-time silver were polished bright; there were flowers in a slender vase, the bread was on an oaken platter carved about with the words, " Give us this day our daily bread," and the sharp knife beside it had a handle of the same wood, smooth at the sides but gracefully carven through and through between. A glance at the table and the room showed that the usually solitary inmate of it was not only daintily neat about everything, but had an eye for grace and the harmony of colors.   Drosée took up the pretty knife and cut another slice of the white bread just for the pleasure of using it.

"It is growing night while I linger here, dear mother of mine !"

" And since Jo is away, there is no need for you to go home. You are to stay all night with me, my daughter. To-morrow I will see about your return. But to-night you need supper and rest after your walk ; and by and by—we can talk."

There was a slight hectic flush on the wan cheek of the mother, and her eyes were bright with excitement. She ate little supper, but assiduously pretended to do so, and urged food upon Drosée until she was fairly obliged to eat heartily.

They talked of the merest trifles, and with an air of great cheerfulness on each side. When they had finished the mother arranged everything on two large trays which she took from a closet, and touched a bell. The kitchen door opened, and a plain-looking middle-aged woman came in, and removed the trays. Then returning, she folded the table-cloth, and spread in its place a table-cover of some Eastern-looking fabric full of dim mingled colors and shot with threads of gold. On this she placed again the quaint, brightly-burning lamp, and was about to withdraw; but turning towards Drosée, who stood by the mantel-piece examining a delicately-painted vase there, she asked:

"Will she be staying here?" .

"Yes, Martha. Put a little more wood on my fire and leave an armful beside it. That is all. Good night."

The servant withdrew, and the mother came up to Drosée and laid a light hand on her shoulder.

"My retinue is dismissed, you see," she said, with one of those smiles which is so ineffably sad when seen to cover a pain or fear on such a worn, fair face. "Come and sit down and tell me—everything, my child."

* * * * * * * *

"He might have waited a little longer yet! It would have been a short time enough! A little longer, for my children's sake! But, O God, must I bear this too?"

The face that had been beautiful Emily Windham's was wan and drawn, the sunken eyes red with passionate weeping, the set mouth all tremulous with uncontrollable pain, as it was lifted in the cruel morning sunshine for an instant, from between two thin, wet hands, towards the far, smiling sky, and was streaming with piteous, helpless tears.

This woman had lived a strange life, between extremes of feeling. Her outward appearance was that of a calmly-melancholy but firmly self-possessed woman. People said of her, "she has had a history, that woman;" but few knew how hard and sad the story. She appeared at times something as she had been in youth—ready, witty, and interesting in conversation; but her prevailing characteristics seemed to be those of a stern, emotionless woman, fervent in religious feeling only.

But the Emily Windham who married John Alwyn was an intelligent, loving, charming young girl, full of enthusiasms, fancies and dreams, though with a stern Calvinistic religious rearing. They had been passionately enamored of each other at first, and even when the differences of moral standards, of aims, and of habits, brought the inevitable roughening to the path of married life, they were still fond and happy at times. By degrees they recognized the lack of perfect sympathy between them; the husband was then fast attaining his brief honors, was popular, worldly, and vanity-struck; the wife lived for her babies, was relentlessly pious and clear-sighted; vexed her husband's false pride daily, and went on to oppose him stanchly in his views of fashionable education and society show for the bright little girls of whom he was more proud than fond. With the years Emily grew apparently colder and sterner, and wore a look of early severity between her matron brows; her passions of lonely weeping and praying and self-upbraidings and questionings were known to no living soul. Her husband's heart was quite alienated; he became more and more neglectful of her, and his attentions to other women became subjects for gossip and even scandal. The crisis came at last in one miserable night; he left her lying face downward in an agony of weeping—left her with a confession of his own unfaithfulness, and a scornful and scorching accusation of her heartlessness as the cause of all. He went to the opera and to supper with his temporary favorite; and when he came home, at three in the morning, his wife was gone.

At first his heart was moved, or his pride touched, so deeply that he was ready to plead, promise, yield anything for the sake of a reconciliation, or even an outward show of peace. He traced the fugitive wife to her retreat; she had gone to an old friend, the lady-principal of a large diocesan school; but she refused to see him. Neither expostulations, rage nor grief had any effect upon her, though they half won the lady, through whom they communicated, to plead his cause. Then followed the last and only cruelty in her husband's power. Since by her cowardly midnight flight from his house she had, he stated, placed herself forever in the wrong, her children should never see her again. She was at that time penniless, wretched, and with a darkened and difficult life before her. She yielded every claim upon her children, and turned herself steadfastly away from the husband whose conduct she felt with a deep and abhorrent resentment; and so began a life forever tormented by a stern and morbidly-indulged remorse, whose outward facts she had told to Drosée at their first meeting; a life unknown to the world, in which strange stories were afloat about her for a time—stories the vain and cruel husband may not have originated, but never confuted, since they left him to play the victim with whatever talent he had—a part he preferred to that of the tyrant, since he lived on the approbation and sympathy of his admirers; and long since the wife was forgotten by the world, which also gradually forgot the unsuccessful author.

John Alwyn had not, however, as to the main facts, deceived this last loving woman whose heart and faith he had won. Jane Ball knew that he had lived miserably with his first wife, that she had left him, that she had refused his overtures for a reconciliation, and that after some time he had quietly obtained a divorce. And knowing all this, Jane Ball was privately married

to him on the morning after that stormy afternoon at
Mrs. Johns' house.

When Drosée drove into Fairvalley in a little
close carriage which was her mother's, and entered the
cottage by the kitchen way, she found the faithful
Jemima bewildered and alone, and was told by her
that her father was married and gone.

" He come in last night and called you all over the
house; he was mad and excited-like when I told him
you was stayin' all night with some of your friends, I
s'posed. He swore like a parrot, and slammed the
door. He was up all night in the study here, and in
and out his room, and this morning he called me and
said: ' Jemima, when the man comes for my trunk, let
him take it. Good-bye; I am going to be married in
fifteen minutes, and I'm going away,' says he. I was
so took back I couldn't breathe a breath; but soon 's
the man took the things, I whipped on my bonnet and
scooted down to the dépôt to watch 'em go, and there
he was, with a lady on his arm, with a big brown vail
over her face, marching up and down the platform.
He caught sight 'n me, dodging around, and called me,
smilin'-like, and says he: ' Jemima, here's my wife; '

'Wish you luck, ma'am,' says I; 'any message for Miss Drosée?' 'None,' says he, very big; and the lady says, 'Tell her——' 'no! no! no! my dear,' says he; and she pulled aside her vail and looked up, and her big blue eyes as asking as a baby's; and then he smiled, and shook his head, and she smiled back at him, and they went away in the train together."

Drosée stood with her face turned away from Jemima as she listened, but her hand lay calmly on the back of a chair near her, and Jemima, observing her quiet, listening attitude, thought that she was bearing it very well. If she had seen Drosée's face, the compressed under-lip and flushed cheek and the strangely lighted dark-blue eyes would have told her that Drosée was more moved and excited than she had ever known her. Suddenly she turned to Jemima, and grasping the hard hands of the old servant, told her that she had just found her mother.

Jemima afterwards related how the shock went to her knees. She sat down and listened in silence, but for a few eloquent exclamations, to the story Drosée told. She had been the children's nurse before their mother left them. In an hour's time Drosée and she had each made up a bundle, put out the fires, set the house in order, locked it up, and gone away together.

Mrs. Windham—as she had long been called—bore the news bravely enough, to all appearance. Drosée had told her enough the night before to prepare her somewhat; it was only when locked in her room, in the solitude she had lived in so long, that the poor wife and mother fell into that passion of piteous weeping, and wildly appealed to God from beneath the latest burden cast upon a broken heart.

For Drosée the trial was of a different nature. It was difficult to subdue a passionate wrath that burned within her, so that in calmness and serenity she might faithfully cheer and help her mother. She felt the impatience of a baffled will, the bitterness of resentment against the inevitable; but her habits of self-control and reasoning enabled her from the first to deny expression to her mortification or her rage; and gradually the fierceness of the struggle was spent, and the grace of serenity came back to the mind and heart of our fair philosopher once more.

*   *   *   *   *   *

At a street corner in New York, on a dull November evening in the week of Mr. Alwyn's departure from Fairvalley, a tall, dark young man, and a tall, blonde young man accidentally met.

"Mr. Seaford! I beg pardon, I have had the pleasure of meeting——"

"Mr. Wilmer! Yes, certainly, we've met at my— in Fairvalley. Glad to see you. Going my way?"

"Thank you—I believe I am, whichever way you are going—unless you are in a hurry."

"Just walking home. It's fine weather for—a cab. But I'm walking for my constitutional," and Louis glanced down with a droll sigh at his round, but still shapely figure, and his lazy blue eyes were lifted only to watch his cane as he twirled it lightly in the air. The two young men turned down the avenue side by side.

There was a striking contrast between them, though both were well-dressed, well-born, well-looking young men in good society. Wilmer was the elder, taller and more extraordinary-looking of the two; his broad, soft black hat was cast carelessly upon his tumbled head, and shaded his massive forehead and noticeably large, dark eyes; his clean-shaven face, with its finely-cut features, thick, dusky locks, a trifle too long for the Northern fashion, his garments, well cut and fine, but loosely worn, and the deliberate, powerful, yet easy stride of his long legs, made altogether an appearance at once unusual and suggestively Southern. Louis Seaford's close blonde locks were cropped convict fashion; his mustache was long and of a tawny gold, his brows fair to whiteness, his blue eyes at once shrewd and mirth-loving, and his round and well-knit figure tightly fitted by the most fashionable garments a Broadway tailor could devise. He was Young New York at its best, for he knew something of literature as well as ledgers, and was well-informed, as well as rich and good-looking. Many girls thought Louis would be the most charming of lovers, and his blonde beauty had touched some tender hearts that knew the best of him as little as they knew Greek; but Wilmer was apter to appeal to the imagination of a woman, and become an object of hero-worship quite unconsciously.

He spoke hesitatingly now to Louis.

"If I may, I should like to ask, Mr. Seaford, if Miss Alwyn is with Mrs. Seaford, your mother?"

"Miss Alwyn?" said Louis, instantly looking more of a business man and less of an idler. "My cousin Drosée? No, she is not with my mother."

"She is not in Fairvalley," said Wilmer, with some slight embarrassment and agitation. "Her friends there are much concerned by her sudden disappearance. My cousin, Mrs. Fielding, desired me to address myself to you for information. I intended to have seen you to-day somehow."

"I can set your mind at rest," Louis said, coolly. "I know where she is. She is all right."

Wilmer bowed, and stood still. Louis's manner seemed to him discourteous; but even at the cost of appearing over-curious he was glad to learn that all was well with Drosée.

"Mrs. Fielding, of course, will hear from her soon," Louis said, immediately. "But I may as well tell *you*, Mr. Wilmer, though at present this is only for you two that Drosée is with her mother."

"Her mother!" Wilmer exclaimed, in astonishment.

"Her mother, who is one of the best women I ever knew," Louis replied, rather haughtily.

"I could never have doubted that Miss Alwyn's mother was so," Wilmer said, quietly.

Something in his tone struck Louis's keen ear, and he guessed rightly how things were with his companion.

"Walk on a bit, will you?" he said, feeling the ready sympathy and respect born of a fellow-feeling. "You know my cousins well, and I may as well relieve my mind when I have a trustworthy listener. You've seen Mr. Alwyn's marriage in the papers?"

"Yes; he was married on Wednesday."

"The two of them sailed for Europe that very day. You know whom he married? She had about five thousand dollars, and he as many hundreds. There's the end of them, as far as I ever want to know. He's my mother's only brother, but even she has given him up at last."

Wilmer's look expressed his attention.

"Drosée's mother has been teaching ever since her separation from her husband. A relation has left her a small property now, and she is living at her childhood's home, a little farm between Brakesburg and Fairvalley. Drosée wrote to me on Wednesday night,

11

and I went out there Thursday. My aunt is a very good woman, but saddened for life. Drosée and she are perfectly wrapped up in each other already. Drosée says she has been wanting her mother all her life, and seems full of delight to be with her again. Perhaps it seems strange to you that it should be so?"

"No. I have heard Miss Alwyn speak of—speak in a manner that would have led me to expect this feeling for her mother," Wilmer said, with apparent composure, but privately annoyed at having let slip even this small admission.

"The deuce you have!" thought Louis. "Well, if Drosée chose to be as confidential as that——"

" I never saw her show as much feeling in my life as she does toward my aunt," he went on. "They are going to be very happy together, I hope, and put aside the remembrance of Mr. Alwyn for the pleasure they find in each other."

"And Miss Jo?" asked Wilmer.

"Oh," said Louis, flushing, "she is not with them. She is in Philadelphia, but she is coming over to spend a few days with them soon. Drosée couldn't tell me when, and I don't know. She went away long before this excitement, and was teaching a friend's children, before we even knew of it here."

"It was very hard for Miss Alwyn to be without her, I should think," Wilmer said, simply.

"Ye–es," Louis answered, with a curious twinkle in his eye. "I don't suppose any one would like to part with—with one's only sister," ending the half-ingenuous speech uncandidly.

Wilmer glanced at Louis, and began to have his own suspicions, in his turn.

"Come in, won't you," asked Louis, pausing at his own door-step. "Do come in, like a good fellow; I haven't had half a talk with you yet."

"Thank you, another time," Wilmer answered, consulting his watch. 'I have promised my cousin to bring her what news I could to-night."

"Well," said Louis, reluctantly, for a great fancy for Wilmer had sprung up within him, "you must go then, I suppose. And we're very quiet here just now; but I should be glad if you'd drop in some time."

"I thank you, Seaford; I'll do so—to-morrow, per·haps, or as that's Sunday——"

"I'll be at home all day after twelve," Louis answered, cheerfully; and so they parted cordially.

As Louis fitted his latch-key in the door, he reflected, however:

"But if I dared to intrude on them, I might run down to Fairvalley to-morrow to see if Jo is there. It won't do, though—it wouldn't do."

Then he carried his handsome face into his mother's richly-furnished room, and the widow put up her fresh, handsome, elderly face to be kissed by him. She was very proud of Louis's filial devotion to her, and leaned on it greatly since his father's death; but the best-considered mother would sometimes be astonished to guess what thoughts are flitting through the brain beneath the dark or light locks she fondly touches; and Louis now, at his mother's feet, looking at her sparkling fire and speaking readily in reply to her remarks, as she smoothed the fair hair just long enough to begin its shorn curves upon his brow, was thinking secretly of the face of his hard young sweetheart, Jo.

CHAPTER IX.

CHRISTMAS-TIDE.

" Yet there is one who seems to be
  Thine elder sister, in whose eyes
A faint, far Northern light will rise
   Sometimes, and bring a dream of thee.
But 'No,' she answers, 'I am she
Whom the gods love, Tranquility.
Who can renounce, and yet endure,
To him I come, not lightly wooed,
But won by silent fortitude.' "

J. R. Lowell.—" Ode to Happiness."

November had passed, December was going. Fair-valley had had little snow or ice as yet, but Christmas was coming, and a new year.

And with Christmas Jo was coming to the Stone Cottage; and on the eve of the new year Trinity Church was going to have a new service; a musical, midnight service, on Sunday night, which was the last night of the year. Several people took the credit of that influence which had moved the church to do this thing; but at any rate, it was to be, for the first time

[245]

in an Episcopal church in Fairvalley; and nobody but
the choir and the rector knew the programme exactly;
but it was to be a solemn service, with chanting and
hymns by the choir, and prayers and portions of Scripture read by Dr. Bampfyle. Drosée's mother had a
piano now at the cottage, and Drosée sometimes shut
herself up and practiced some melancholy music or
other.

She had robbed Fairvalley of its hoped-for mystery
and budding sensation by quietly taking her place in
the choir on the Sunday morning after that Wednesday on which the rumor of her father's private marriage and her disappearance had set the town agog; it
was now understood that she was living near Fairvalley
with her mother, and by this time her few friends
had been welcomed at the cottage. Mrs. Johns had
come timidly, and been received kindly. She had
been a great admirer of Emily Windham in her
youth, and much more simple and uneducated than her
country neighbor; but she came, and was received as
a friend now, and the unaffected goodness of her heart
re-won the regard of her old acquaintance.

Dr. Stark came, by invitation, and not seldom after

that. To Mrs. Windham he was her daughter's literary sponsor, and Dr. Stark was careful never to touch on any religious topics in her presence. He saw, and perhaps he only, that there was a lack of a perfect understanding between the mother and daughter, who had lived apart so long, and he did nothing to make it apparent.

And in truth, Drosée had now lost her latest illusion. She had her mother at last, and they loved each other; but perfect joy is to be found in attaining no material desire she still was forced to hold. Her mother and she secretly differed in all their thoughts and feelings. The mother's life had rendered her religion into a kind of account book between herself and her God; she never suffered without torturing her conscience to seek out the frailty or sin she was being punished for; rewards and punishments, strictly meted, here and hereafter, was the firmest idea she had of an Almighty Ruler; and Drosée learned (from a conversation they once had) that she must never dare to assail her mother's convictions; for the only effect that her exposition of a belief in God as love, her quoted saying that since " an inert, unintelligent or malevolent love is simply a contradiction in terms," " love, if it means anything, means good-will acting freely with a wise and intelligent design," was met by the grave reply that God revealed himself not only as a father, but as a judge, to whom vengeance belongeth, and a difference in the interpretation of that text brought forth in the heart-wearied and soul-sick mother, whose struggle with life had left her fixed in a bitter sense of her own blame-worthiness before God and man, a passion of tears, every drop of which seemed to burn on Drosée's heart; and a wailing cry that " this was her punishment, her punishment; her own child, whom she had deserted, had fallen into easy and dangerous doctrines of salvation, and her mother was to blame for it." Our gentle young philosopher soothed her as best she could; and from that day she had lived under the strain of physical nearness to one who is far away; she had felt that her mother grieved and prayed for her in secret; and had at times felt impelled to dissemble in order to please her; and so the days went by.

The mother, on her part, was striving to do every outward thing for her beloved daughter's happiness. She received such company as came to them, cordially;

her gentle and gracious manners and attempts at good cheer were infinitely lovely and touching; the tenderest affection was in both hearts, but there was a vail between them never to be lifted.

Louis came down on a second visit to them a few days before Christmas. Mrs. Windham looked more pale and wan than usual that evening, but she was very courteous and friendly to Louis, whom she liked; and when she rose to retire early, asking to be excused because of a headache, Louis insisted on carrying her lamp up-stairs for her, and having set it on a table just within her door, astonished her by turning gently to her, taking both of her hands, and saying:

"Aunt Emily, are you in any trouble I can help you out of? Please call on me as if I were your son," he concluded hastily, blushing like a boy. The dark-eyed lady looked keenly at him an instant, smiled faintly, sighed, and said kindly:

"I need nothing but rest, dear boy. Good-night, my son," and then Louis kissed her wan cheek with a boy's impulsiveness, but a man's sincere respectfulness, and went down-stairs with an unusually sober face.

Drosée was alone by the fire. He sat down by her

11*

and quietly took her hand. This being a not unheard-of, though rather unusual, familiarity between the cousins, Drosée permitted it serenely, and merely looked at him with gentle inquiry. She knew Louis was going to be confidential when he took her hand and looked serious.

"Drosée," he began abruptly, "did Jo tell you about us last summer?"

" About—us ?"

" About my asking her to marry me ?"

"Louis Seaford!   Is that true ?"

"Hard-hearted little soul! So she was even ashamed to tell you ?"

"Ashamed! I don't think Jo ever did anything to be ashamed of in her life," said Drosée valiantly. "But this is true; for the first time that I know of, she has kept a secret from me." She stopped, bewildered. "And what did you do, Louis?"

" Tried it twice, and then went away and tried to bear my fate like a man."

" Poor boy! Dear Louis, I am so sorry! You would be the most agreeable of brothers."

" Thank you, dear," squeezing the hand he held,

and frowning with the gravity of thought. "But, Drosée, I can't make up my mind to be pitied; I want her yet. I was so sure she did love me. Do *you* think she doesn't?"

"I am afraid she doësn't, Lou," reluctantly.

"Is there any one else?" Louis asked, sitting bolt upright in dismay.

"I am not clear that I have anything to say," Drosée returned, as diplomatically as possible.

"Oh, heavens! If that's it—" poor Louis said, dropping his face between his hands. Drosée was touched. She had a sincere affection for Louis, and she had never known him so frankly distressed in her life. She put her hand on his shoulder. He looked up presently, with quite a haggard expression, and an agitated air.

"See here, Drosée," he said, speaking rapidly. "I can't think Jo is a flirt. And I tell you this, I came and told her I was coming to stay in Fairvalley while you were away with my people—that is, if you would go—and she as good as owned to me that she staid at home because of my being here; I had frankly told her I came on *her* account."

Drosée looked troubled, and shook her head.

"Remember the night she went out and walked with me, and we only came home when we saw the light in your room—you had come back from a club-meeting or something? She promised me then to tell you she wouldn't go away. She gave me a rose—I've got it now—she let me put it in her hair early in the evening."

Drosée bent her looks on the fire, and bit her lip thoughtfully.

"She—she—I can't tell you, and I *won't* tell you," said the young man, starting up, and a blush rising to his fair and manly cheek at the idea of betraying Jo further, even to her sister, by relating the favors that had been modestly yielded as to a cousin, but which had thrilled them both with a deeper meaning—"but she did not love any other man *then*, Drosée, and I'll swear it by her own pure heart!"

"Louis, I have been mistaken, I have been mistaken!" Drosée cried, rising, too. "I see it now: she made one half-confession to me; and I thought it was some one else, not knowing that you were to be in Fairvalley. I know she staid for some one's sake; I believe now it was for yours; and if Jo loved you once, she'll love you forever!"

"God bless you!—who did you think it was?" Louis asked.

"I cannot tell you. It would be unjust to her to do it—fastening my folly on her."

"But I won't misunderstand. Only tell me, that I may laugh at it. Was it—was it any of the teachers in that Sunday-school?"

"No, no—but——"

"Was it—ah!—Drosée, was it"—whispering—" *Wilmer,* perhaps?"

Drosée's blush was so swift a reply to more questions than one that Louis impetuously caught her in his arms, and laughed softly and triumphantly as she extricated herself from them, pale now as she had been red.

"That is all right," he said confidently.

"Then why did she refuse you twice?" Drosée asked hastily.

Louis looked sober.

"It was my fault," he said, "at least, I think and hope so. Drosée, I shall try again. May I come over at Christmas, and will you just give me a chance when you can?"

"I will promise that. But can you leave Aunt Mary—or will she come if I write and ask her? Or——"

"Oh, she will spend Christmas at my grand-father's. I don't think I *need* her here, exactly," he said, with a conscious blush. "That will be all right afterwards. Don't tell Jo I'm coming, will you? I want to surprise her."

And this he effectually did, a week later.

Jo had come, looking a little paler, and a little heavier about the eyes than of old, but bright and pretty Jo still. She would not hear any talk of her breaking her engagement for the year's work; she had vetoed that on her first visit to her mother. She pretended not to think it honorable; she really was resolved not to be in Fairvalley, where Louis could naturally see her often without any definite seeking of her. She would never be in his way again, by her own will. Perhaps she had longed sometimes for him to come to her in those three months away from home; certain it is that she had never ceased to think of him in his grief over his father's death-bed, his care that followed, his apparently relentless silence—a silence really longer in seeming to her than to him, for Louis had less leisure than she, and more hope and power as to the ending of their estrangement.

Jo came home, then, with a proud and stubborn, yet loving heart, and talked to Drosée and her mother of everything under the sun but the little ache down at the root of all pleasure and action ; and they, who had each other's confidence, did not say a word to her of Louis' coming. They sent her down to the parlor to finish a wreath of evergreens for its decoration, alone, while they delayed for some plausible reason up-stairs, but really looked out of the window for Louis; and the first Jo knew of him, he had silently entered the fire-lit room in the gathering twilight.

"Merry Christmas !" cried Jo bravely, jumping up, dropping the evergreens, and holding out her hand.

"Will you add to that a Happy New Year?" asked Louis, who had been wondering what words he should find to woo Jo in, and who now found them readily enough. The tone in which he spoke was sufficiently significant, and Jo's up-flashing eyes saw a serious and tender look in his that she could not well meet. She looked down; and Louis added simply, "Jo, you have my life in your hands. I shall be miserable if you cannot pity me."

There was a long silence. Jo did not withdraw her hand from his, though he held it lightly and deferentially.

"Will you ask only pity?" asked Jo at last, very low.

"I beg for love," said Louis, coming closer. Jo sank back into her chair, and Louis dropped on his knee at her side. He took nothing, though she was submissive enough now; only he still held the little hand; and when Jo bent forward he put his cheek to hers. A whisper did the rest, and Jo was won forever.

"And what have you besides love to go upon?" the mother asked, holding Jo's radiant young face between her thin, white palms that night, and looking with sad and loving eyes into the lovely young life sparkling there.

"Is not love enough?" said Jo, happily.

"No, my child, not enough. To make married life

happy, there must be sympathy, understanding and trust; similar aims and beliefs."

" *That* I call love," Jo said. " The—the attraction between us includes all that."

"Sure, my darling ?"

"Sure, mother!—We are *made* to be happy together," Jo went on, blushing vividly. " We love the same things—we like to do the same things—we care for each other's happiness—we want to be true to others and to—to God ;—don't *you* believe we will be happy, mother ?"

" You have a fair chance, dear," the mother said, with a satisfied look replacing the anxious one an instant. " And now, good-night, and sleep well; to-morrow is Christmas day, you know."

" Merry Christmas, mother ?"

" The merriest for many a long year, dear child."

" Drosée, *did* you think I was in love with Mr. Wilmer ?" Jo asked, her head pillowed on Drosée's arm that night.

" Forget that now," Drosée said, in a muffled voice. And long after Jo was lost in happy dreams, Drosée lay awake, thinking. By and by she rose, and went softly into her mother's room, to see if she slept. Yes, and heavily; but again the pillow was wet with tears.

Drosée came back to her own room, and sat alone by the window.

"My life is not without its best value yet," she thought. "The vanity of desire is proven; love is no more mine; my will and my anger have been futile, and all outward successes slip away from me. The best of everything is yet mine; the willingness to perceive and know my duty, and the one purpose, faithfully to fulfill it to my life's last day."

That "progress in virtue is a greater good than the mere attainment of happiness," who can gainsay? Disappointment and loss are weak before a soul so armed. And Drosée slept at last, a disciplined, tried and conquering heart at the end of a long march.

CHAPTER X.

NEW YEAR'S EVE.

Epicurus.—I would never think of death as an embarrassment, but a blessing.

Fernissa.—How a blessing ?

Epicurus.—What if it make our enemies cease to hate us?
What if it make our friends love us the more?

W. S. LANDOR.

SUNDAY night, the 31st of December, a "midnight
mass for the dying year" was being held in Trinity
Church at Fairvalley. The light streamed out from
the high, narrow windows of the weather-beaten old
edifice upon the deep, fresh-fallen snow, with the
whitest radiance. The church was filled and packed
long before half-past eleven, the time for the service
to begin ; everybody had been drawn forth by the
novelty, even the members of St. Luke's Church,
though their pastor was decidedly disposed to scoff at
this innovation, and was not present.

As Dr. Bampfyle, in black robes, entered the
chancel, the organ first sounded, and music filled the

[259]

listening ears of the breathless mass of people. Now collects had been read, solemn portions of the psalms chanted, and a brief address made; and through the silent church came a clear, soft, warning voice, as if it fell from a spirit land; Drosée Alwyn was singing all alone—

> " Days and moments quickly flying,
> Blend the living with the dead ;
> Soon must you and I be lying,
> Each within a narrow bed."

Mrs. Windham, Louis and Jo were in Mrs. Johns' pew. They moved, softly, and added their upturned gaze to that from hundreds of other eyes that were fastened on the pure white face of the singer standing in the center of the choir. Two other gazers stood unnoted not far away. One was Dr. Stark, and one was a tall, dark figure in the shadow of the gallery; Wilmer had come out to Fairvalley that night with his friend, solely to attend this famous service. Not even Louis knew of his presence; and Drosée he never meant to know of it. She sang on, hundreds of eyes riveted on her, apparently without other emotion than that of deep and awed feeling.

> " Jesu, Infinite, Redeemer,
>   Maker of this mortal frame,
> Teach, Oh, teach us to remember
>   What we are, and whence we came !
>
> Whence we came, and whither wending;
>   Soon we must through darkness go,
> To inherit bliss unending,
>   Or eternity of woe."

Then the full-toned choir joined in chanting:

> " As the tree falls, so must it lie:
> As the man lives, so will he die:
> As the man dies, such must he be
> All through the days of eternity."

In the silent pause that followed, the clergyman knelt, and the congregation bent forward almost unanimously for the two or three minutes left for silent prayer; the gas dimmed down; and then the bell tolled slowly—twelve slow strokes—and the church burst into new life; the lights flared, the doors were being opened and shut by an irreverent few, among whom was Mr. Manton Estwick, who wished to avoid the later crush in out-pouring; there was noise, and bright light, stir, and cool air rushing in ; and the choir had burst forth into a jubilant singing of the " Gloria in Excelsis," the last of the service.   But in the midst of it broke forth sounds of dismay and terror; the lights had been turned up too high, or been too much swayed by the current of air; some white paper flowers and the more inflammable portions of the Christmas decorations were ablaze in several places, and the light wood-work about the choir railing, the slight wooden cross covered with dry grasses, just above the gas, and even the curtains of the choir were on fire as if by magic.

The horrors of the moments that ensued were those of every such cruel and cowardly panic. People fought madly for dear life; some were crushed and beaten under foot, some fainting, some shrieking, and here and there blazing bits of wood fell. Every one knew the church to be old, and dry as tinder; the windows were high from the ground, the doors narrow; it was a terrible moment for many.

Louis Seaford's presence of mind did not for an instant desert him.

"Sit down! Sit down!" he cried in clear and commanding tones to those about him. "There is plenty of time. Sit down." His own party obeyed, and a few near him wavered, paused, and sat down too. They were near the front. The maddened crowd surged by them, and then Louis took Jo's arm with one hand, and Mrs. Windham's with the other.

"This way," he said, quietly, and led them straight forward, through the small vestry door, and out at the rear of the church, followed by Mr. and Mrs. Johns, and some few others, safe and unhurt.

"Drosée! Drosée!" cried Mrs. Windham, wildly, turning back to the church.

"I'll go for her," said Louis, coolly, restraining her. "Jo—stay quiet, darling. I will come back."

He re-entered the church, and smoke rolled through the door just after. Mrs. Windham broke from Jo's hold with a sudden vehemence, and crying again in an agony the name of her favorite child, ran toward the church. Mr. Johns caught her back, and Jo clasped her in her arms again; her mother tried to speak, raised a wavering hand, and sunk heavily against Jo's breast, with blood springing from between her pale lips.

Meanwhile there had been others to remember Drosée. Dr. Stark and his companion had both of them thought of her before themselves. Leaping upon a seat, Dr. Stark saw that the members of the choir had deserted the little gallery, flying down the narrow stairs, and probably struggling now for freedom with the living mass packed against the little door at the foot.

He cried aloud, in his harsh, strident voice:

"Open the gallery door!" and pressed wildly forward, as if with his bent and puny body he could force sense or obedience into that surging crowd.

But Wilmer paused, and looked about him; then leaped into the chancel, and with the raging strength born of desperation, tore a stout oaken chair apart, and with a mighty brand in his strong arm, leaped forward, tall, athletic, and with the resistless dash of a madman, broke through the crowd, through which, ere it closed upon him, the doctor's feebler figure pressed. It took a determined and manful fight, with that weapon in hand, to reach and clear a space sufficient to open the gallery door; that done, a dozen figures broke forth; the stairs were tottering and licked by flames even now, but the crowd was rapidly melting away. Wilmer rushed up the gallery stair, and at its top, in the smoke, stumbled on a fainting figure, and heard the music of a voice he knew.

"Oh, can you lift her? She has fainted, and they have left her," Drosée cried, not knowing to whom she spoke.

"Are *you* safe?" cried Dr. Stark, at Wilmer's heels.

"Quite. Save this poor woman first." Dr. Stark seized Drosée's arm, but she hung back until Wilmer had bent his strength to lift the fallen figure before him; and he, going down the stairs in advance of them, bore into the reviving air the passive bulk of Drosée's bitter enemy, Mrs. Manton Estwick.

The other two were nearly at the foot of the stairs, when the steps gave way entirely, and, hurled to the floor, they were suddenly overwhelmed in the collapse and crush of timber.

It was not long—it was doubtless not a minute—before Louis, coming forth from the smoky air of the church, supporting an old man he had found helpless there and brought out to the free air of heaven again, and Wilmer, re-entering in dismay to search for the two missing—having delivered Mrs. Estwick to her husband, who had been looking for her in the crowd —discovered what had happened. Together they

12

cleared away the débris from above these two, and lifted them out. Dr. Stark had been struck and momentarily stunned by a falling beam which had slanted above him, and chiefly protected him from the rain of smaller missiles ; but Drosée lay face downward under a heap of loose timber, laths, and plastering, and was either suffocated, or from some other cause unconscious, and Wilmer bore her through the yawning doors, lying lifelessly upon his breast.

In the early dawn of that sad New Year's day, Wilmer lifted his heavy eyes to the pale and grief-marked face of Louis, who, with dishevelled hair and a tear-stained cheek, had entered the parlor of Mrs. Johns' villa, where Wilmer sat.

"Forgive me that I have left you alone so long," Louis said, in a voice he tried hard to control ; "I could not——"

Wilmer waved the apology aside with a gesture.

"What news?" he asked, in the low tone of one grimly resolved to know the sentence of fate.

"My aunt is sinking fast ; there is no hope."

"And Miss Alwyn?" Wilmer asked, in the same suppressed voice.

"And Drosée—we fear—cannot long survive her."

Wilmer's dark cheek turned pale, his lips and eyelids contracted, and his hands clinched; he uttered not a syllable, but turned away to the closed window, and leaned there in dumb and moveless grief. Louis went to him, and putting his arm on Wilmer's shoulder, stood beside him with an unutterable, silent sympathy, the tears overflowing his eyes; he bowed his head on his arm, and gave vent for a moment to unaffected grief.

"Seaford, is there no hope?" said Wilmer, after a pause, in a deep voice. "*Why* cannot she live? What is the injury? Can no one do anything?"

"Her arm is badly broken, and she no sooner revives than she loses consciousness, as if with pain. The doctor does not think it prudent to attempt to set her arm at present; he seems to be afraid that she is more injured than we can tell. I don't know anything about his business, Wilmer, but he does seem to me more timid and uncertain than a practical physician should be; yet they say he is the best here; I may do him injustice ignorantly."

"Seaford," said Wilmer, with a faint gleam of light

in his eyes, "if there is any doubt—do not think me intrusive—but there *is* a surgeon near here—old Kennedy, of New York, of whom you have heard—he retired, and came to this neighborhood two or three years ago to recruit his health; he is living on his own place near Brakesburg. Let me go for him. I know him well. He made a great cure for my grandfather a few years since. I can fetch him to Miss Alwyn, if you consent."

"Do you think so?"

"I will. Alive or dead, he shall be brought," said Wilmer impetuously, turning to go. "Don't refuse your consent—he ought to come and see her, at least."

"I empower you with whatever authority I have," Louis said. "How will you go? it is beginning to rain. Have you your overcoat?"

"I will be back within two hours," said Wilmer, pulling his hat about his eyes. "Good-bye, Seaford, till I come—and—and—you will not *let* her die?"

And so, with a lover's haste, this eager messenger departed from the door of Mrs. Johns' pretty villa, where the dying lay, and went on his doubtful errand.

An hour later, life in the mother's breast ebbed

down to the last retreating wave, and went out with a whispering sigh. Her fearful, humble and penitent spirit, which had so sorely suffered in this world, passed away to the next with a calm and trustful confidence which seemed unearthly; and the heavenly light in the eyes which had wept their latest tears lingered on the serene face when it was cold forever.

When Wilmer returned, in the morning light, there sat beside him in the buggy a stout, elderly man with a fine, resolute, and benevolent face, whose very aspect inspired confidence.

"There has been a death here," said Dr. Kennedy, as they drew up at the gate.

For an instant Wilmer, about to descend, paused, struck to the heart with dread; then he leaped from the buggy and hurried to the door, from which already fluttered the vail of crape. It was opened ere he reached it by a servant.

"Mr. Seaford?" Wilmer asked. It was the only name he could utter.

"He is with his cousin, sir. Her mother died this morning."

"*Her* mother?—Miss Drosée, is——"

"Oh, I beg pardon, sir, you are the gentleman brought her out of the fire. Please walk in, sir. Miss Drosée is not much altered since daybreak. She is conscious just now."

"Doctor, come in, sir," said Wilmer, turning about to the rather neglected old gentleman, who had been left to help himself out of the buggy, and tie his horse. There was a wonderful light in his face, and a certain thrill in his voice which belonged to unexpressed thanksgiving. "Tell Mr. Seaford that Dr. Kennedy is with me, please, and—and come this way, sir."

"Is the doctor in charge still here?" asked the old gentleman, pausing, and turning to the servant. "Yes!—Ah—I must ask to see him at once, Mr. Wilmer, before I presume to interfere with his patient."

And then came professional courtesies and consultations, and after some delay, Wilmer's surgeon went up-stairs with the doctor.

For days after Drosée's arm had been safely set, she lingered so near the border-land between this and the unknown world that every heart that loved her was tried to the uttermost by fear and suspense. And many people who had so lately been ready to deny all favor, both to her mother and to her, had been moved by the sudden close of Emily Windham's unhappy career; and her sad and pure life, her goodness and beauty, were talked of with a gentle and pitiful feeling. The snow lying above her new grave hid not more purely the broken earth than the love of those who had known her best covered her faults and errors with the close and spotless vail of charity. "What if it makes our friends love us the more?"

And Drosée, traveling in the valley of the shadow, had her journey noted by those who had disliked her only less anxiously than by those who had loved her long. Death's lifted finger had put to silence the strife and clamor of tongues. Mrs. Estwick, who knew now who had saved her, had deeper cause than any to repent of the evil done to a young and gentle woman, whose only social sin had been that she had been singular in some of her ideas, and attractive to some for whom she had not cared greatly. And however people might hereafter esteem Drosée living, sure it was that dying her loveliness and wit and wisdom would be remembered and praised in Fairvalley long after many esteemed more orthodox were forgotten by their world.

And to Mrs. Johns, that ever-gentle servitor by the sick-bed ; to Jo's faithful heart; to Louis' brotherly love ; to the many who loved Drosée, scattered far and near, what did death teach of her?

To them all, much as they had loved her, came a new keenness and depth of feeling, understanding, memory. To Wilmer, the prospect of losing her forever betrayed how little he had resigned himself to that decision she had indicated to him when he first ventured to hint to her of his feeling ; he remembered her in all the beauty and charm of the first days of their swiftly-advancing friendship ; her bravery in peril, her serenity in pain ; the old words and ways came back ; the same light flame of hope sprang up again within him, and died down again ; the same words trembled on his tongue and were unspoken ; the touch of a small hand lingered so palpably upon his palm that he could almost hope to close his fingers and clasp it there again ; and this passion was so blended with pain, this tenderness with dread, that its sweetness was an anguish—yet an anguish he would not have yielded in change for ignorance of its power.

Ah, "What if it makes our enemies cease to hate us? What if it makes our friends love us the more?"

12*

CHAPTER XI.

IN THE DAWN.

> " Thy grandeur is the shade we seek,
> To be eternal is Thy use to us;
> Ah, Blessed God! what joy it is to me
> To lose all thought of self in Thine eternity!"
>
> F. W. FABER.

" DEAR Jo!"

" Drosée, are you awake?"

"I do not sleep much, do I? I have been thinking of so many things this evening, Jo, I want to talk. Sometimes I want to speak, and cannot; I cannot open eyes or lips."

"You are very weak. It is the fever, darling; you will be stronger soon."

Jo's pitiful, loving voice had a slight tremor in it. Drosée, who had dropped her eyelids again, raised them, and looked earnestly at the fair young face near her. Her eyes looked larger and more brilliant than

[274]

ever, her face was so wan. She gazed at Jo in silence with that long, long look which the dying sometimes have, all life seeming concentrated in their eyes. Jo bore the look as long as she could, and then her under-lip began to tremble like a child's, in spite of herself.

"Don't cry, Jo," said Drosée, breaking silence. "I want to believe that you will go with a smile through life. We were so different; my very name has a hint in it of tears. Do not let it mean tears to you."

"It is not 'tears,' it is 'dew,'" said Jo, with an effort to regain her composure. "You have been a blessing to me, and will always be."

"Then promise me to think reasonably and calmly of me by and by, darling. If I know anything—if I individually exist—I shall care to know that you are happy."

"Drosée, do not talk like that! You will know how I am, because you will see me every day; you will live with Louis and me. When you get better we have so much to arrange about everything," and Jo smiled cheerfully.

"I shall never live to get better, Jo; you must not talk to me as if I were a child to be deceived, or a coward to fear change. I am not afraid to die. I have thought of it very pleasantly at times. Do you not care—may you not care sometimes, to know how I feel now?"

"Maybe," faltered Jo. "But I hope the time is very far——"

"If you cry, I cannot talk, my poor Jo."

"I will not cry."

"Jo, I have been lying here looking back on my life. It looks—it looks—it looks most like a winding river, I think; mist rising, and the dawn above it; there is a faint light on its flow; and one by one the lamps on it go out, because it is near day."

The feverish glow on the cheek, the rare fluency of speech, cause Jo's heart to quake.

"It seems to me I have been learning all my life to give up. The last thing to resign is the love of life. The lights go out one by one, but the mists are rising. I believe that flush is dawn. I named these lights, lying here: that unresting flame of desire; that false beacon, fame; that pale, love of ease; that windy light, of popularity; that angry glow, of will and pride; love, with its flickering torch; and more—I think they were all blown out—because the dawn was near."

The low, musing, beautiful voice paused; its cadences had been like those of one who softly hums a song, or reads a beloved poem. Drosée had written poems; but none had ever sounded so sweetly strange and pathetic to Jo as this last one, softly uttered.

"Oh, Drosée, how can you be so calm? I cannot, cannot understand! Drosée, can you be quite willing to die?"

"If you were dying, should you rebel, Jo?"

"If it were God's will—I'd try not—not to rebel; but I am afraid I could not help it; with all its pain, life is too sweet to me."

"With Louis—yes; and you are young, and strong, and good! But, Jo, I feel it slip away and cannot wish it to linger. I don't know; the last renunciation is not hard; even personal existence I can yield up at last."

"Oh, Drosée, don't! my dear, do you mean that—as you said—you don't feel sure of life beyond?"

"Of life—yes. Of personal life I know nothing.

It does not matter to me; I have never tried to be convinced of it."

"But, my dear, it is so easy to see that it is true. Drosée, let me show you—or let me send for Dr. Bampfyle. You must let him teach you of it."

"I am willing, dear. But it does not matter. Dr. Bampfyle has been to see so many sick people lately. And I shall know all soon."

"Drosée, my darling, don't! Darling, what are you hoping for? What can make you tranquil when you think of entering the other life, and it is so dark?"

"It is not dark," Drosée answered, in a weary voice. "God, who is Love, fills it. To be near him, or absorbed in him—that is heaven."

"But others, darling? Drosée—do you not *want* to live as yourself—to see and know our mother, Drosée, and those dear to us?--that would be half of heaven to me."

Drosée turned her large, heavy eyes toward the window.

"I want to know that they are blessed, if I know anything: but for her and you—God will care best."

Jo was silent, touching the wan hand caressingly, for a time, and Drosée too had ceased to speak, closing her eyes; at last Jo said, in an awed and gentle voice:

"It is a land of clouds to me. How can you long to enter it?"

"Because I love the life I sprang from, Jo," said Drosée, in a tender, mild, faint voice. "How can I fear? Love created us and disposes of us. That is all I feel. Somehow—somewhere—I shall find— God."

The voice of this fair philosopher sunk into silence, and the silence was unbroken. Jo bent to her presently, with a sick, short thrill of speechless dread; but she was breathing, very faintly, but calmly and naturally; she was in a quiet slumber.

CHAPTER XII.

THE LIGHT OF DAY.

"Invisible hands may gird thy armor on,
And Nature put new weapons in thy hand,
Sending thee out to try the world again—
Perchance to conquer, being cased in mail
Of double memories."—E. C. STEDMAN.

"Whatever is taught or told,
However men moan or sigh,
Love never shall grow cold,
And Life shall never die."
—BAYARD TAYLOR.

FANNY FIELDING, sitting in her rose-shaded room, with her soft-breathing baby asleep in the cradle near, dropped into her lap the ribbon she had been twisting into loops and bows, and looked around, hearing her husband's cautious step upon the stair. This was one of her first "sitting-up" days, and she awaited his pleased surprise with a smile. Mr. Fielding had nearly lost his wife in her recent illness, and his love and care for her had been renewed wondrously. They had begun their first truly happy year together.

[280]

After the first greetings and the half shy caresses the gray-haired husband bestowed on his still young and very pretty wife, Fanny asked:

"Have you seen Wilmer to-day?"

"Yes, he is coming up by and by to dinner."

"Did he say how Drosée was?"

"He sent you word only yesterday that she was better, dear."

"You are sure she is not worse again, then?"

"He had not seen Seaford to-day, but he probably will before he comes up. He said he would be here by five if he didn't conclude to go down to Fairvalley with Stark to-night."

"Poor fellow! He is in a great state of anxiety, no doubt."

"You choose to think so, my little match-maker. He seems much as usual to me. Are you so certain that he was ever smitten there?"

"I am perfectly certain."

"Be it so, my dear. Hark! There's the bell now."

In a moment a servant tapped at the door, and delivered to Mr. Fielding a note. He handed it to his wife.

It contained Wilmer's regrets. He was called out of town. "Please say to Mrs. Fielding that her friend is decidedly better."

Mrs. Fielding glanced from this demure note to her husband's face, at first meditatively, then with a dawning smile of triumph. He understood it, laughed good-naturedly, and pinched her fair, round cheek.

Several days before this Drosée had been pronounced convalescent, and, still lying on her bed, weak and wan from pain and fever, she doubtfully, slowly, recognized the fact that she was very possibly to recover.

She did not talk much, but avoided speech even with Jo; she suffered little, was usually obedient in trying to eat and sleep, and mended a little daily. But so slight was this gradual improvement that Jo was disheartened.

"I can't tell what to do for her," she said to Louis. "She never asks for anything; she never seems to care for anything; I think she had so made up her mind to dying that she doesn't get accustomed to living."

"It is weakness," Louis suggested, caressing Jo's pretty hand.

"No, it is—indifference," Jo said. "I worried her to talk to-day, and she said that she was trying to adapt herself to her conditions; that she perceived herself strangely weak and ignorant; as long as our mother lived, she would have felt the special duty as a special reason for living; and then two great tears swam into her eyes, and we did not talk any more."

Neither did Louis talk any more for a few minutes; he kissed the tears out of Jo's own brimming eyes.

"Jo," he said, after a while, "do you know, I'm inclined to try a remedy on Drosée I don't believe any other woman but you would respond to—be a little selfish, apparently. Talk to her about yourself, by degrees, and our plans, and how we are waiting for her recovery to take her home with us and have the happiest, quietest little wedding ever was. It 'll bring her round; you'll see."

"But, Louis, what an effort for her! I couldn't expect it of her."

"It will do her good, my dearest little Jo, and I'll answer for it. Drosée is true grit you know, when she's tested. Promise me to be happy, darling, and to seem so when you are with her. She'll rise to it."

The proposal did credit to the head and the heart of the young diplomat. Jo adopted his plan, and Drosée made the effort he anticipated. She put aside her own thoughts and discouragement, half-marveling, but wholly pleased, at Jo's radiant and eager happiness, and fell in with all Jo's plans.

"I can sit up to-day, I think," she said, one morning; and the next day,

"Mrs. Johns, let me leave my room and go across to yours this morning. I must get strong—Jo is so happy and hopeful," she added, with a tender little smile, when alone with her old friend.

"I have been presumptuous," she had said to herself, when thinking silently alone. "I thought I had passed through the worst. I find now that the hardest thing of all is to face a life one does not cling to. I am obliged to live with wider and more impersonal interests; to be trained to larger charity and unselfish service. I begin to see my ignorance, and guess my lesson. I am willing to live and learn it—but I can't—I can't feel the proper enthusiasm for it !"

But now, a call upon her for active unselfishness coming, she had ceased thinking so much about it, and found doing more natural. When she went down stairs first, she smiled out of the depths of her easy-chair at Jo, and said, cheerily:

"If there is one thing about which you are more despotic than another, it is pen and ink, Jo; but, an't please you, I'd like to write to Fanny Fielding to-day."

"You will have to use my pen if you do," Jo said; "I have instituted a secret search for yours lately, but——"

"It is lost?"

"I should say," Jo returned, "that, as it is no-where, it has evidently passed in Nirvâna."

"Now do something desperate and expressive, Drosée," Louis suggested. "I know you cherished that pen!"

"Dr. Stark gave it to me," Drosée said, simply. "When did you see Dr. Stark, Louis?"

"Yesterday. He asked for you, as usual. We were on the same train, and he was growling at the public generally. He says people don't want news, nowadays, they want sensations!"

Drosée laughed, and Louis' eyes lit up at the sound.

"He is very anxious to see you again," the young man went on. "And you must let him come in soon. And when will you see the man who saved your life, Drosée? Wilmer's old long face, while you were so ill, used to haunt me night and day."

"*Who* saved me?" Drosée asked, with a new ring to her voice.

"Well, Wilmer tore things to pieces trying," Louis said. "If you hadn't made him carry out that old woman ahead of you, you'd have been all right now. As it was, he dug you out from under the lumber that was above you, and brought you to this house in his own arms."

Drosée was very pale.

"Now, don't look like that," Louis said, glancing about for a fan. "I've kept them from talking about this by the doctor's orders, for fear of exciting you; and now I'll say no more till the color in your face is a little livelier, my dear."

"Oh, I am very well," Drosée said, the color flu hing her delicate cheek. "Tell me—tell me everything."

"Well, there's not much more to tell. He kept a midnight vigil in this parlor for hours, during which not a soul went near him, until I came and told him you were like to die; and then he got on a horse and galloped off in the storm and sleet and brought the surgeon who set your arm, and, in my opinion, saved you."

"When did you see *him*, Louis?" Drosée asked gently, after a moment's hesitation.

"I see him every day. When I didn't go to the city daily he used to run out here at night, to see Stark, and come and ask for you. We feel free to draw our own conclusions, you know."

"You may conclude that he is a loyal friend, and that I am deeply grateful to him," Drosée replied, quickly.

"You personified pride! I didn't suppose you'd think him worthy to be anything more," Louis retorted, artfully.

"I think him worthy of anything," Drosée said,

quite proudly, lifting her dark blue eyes with a life in them more vivid and strong than had shone there in long weeks. "But admiration and gratitude are not—not what Jo feels for you, dear boy!"

The words were brave enough, and Louis forbore to annoy her. But a day or two later he told her Wilmer had come down to Fairvalley. Should he go to the hotel after tea and bring him up?

"Yes—and Dr. Stark, please," Drosée said, with a firm, even voice.

It was growing dark. Jo and Louis had gone out for a walk, and Mrs. Johns had not come down-stairs. Drosée, alone in the warm and silent parlor, walked up and down it a little restlessly, and then sat down near the window.

Presently she saw a tall figure walking alone beyond the low fence and the leafless trees. An impatient hand, with the old trick she knew so well, took off the wide black hat for a moment, and the strong, dark face was turned inquiringly toward the house. She sprang up involuntarily, and in an instant saw that her movement had been seen. Wilmer turned about, hurriedly opened the gate, and came with rapid strides up the path. Trembling, Drosée unfastened the long window, and attempted to open it. A muscular hand from the outside raised it swiftly, and with a glow on his cheek and an eager light in his eyes, Wilmer was at her side. Clasping her hand in his, he turned about and closed the window behind them; then taking her other hand gently, he led her nearer the dancing fire, and pausing, looked down at her with delight.

She was all in white, as he had first seen her, but the white was of a heavy, warm, and clinging woolen stuff; she was thin, but the rare, deep blue eyes were full of kindness, and the soft brown hair waved and clung in the old graceful curves about her head.

"Look at me," said Wilmer, softly, as her eyes fell before his own. He stood holding her two hands together between his.

She looked up, for a second's space.

"Be my friend!" she said, in a tremulous voice. He saw that she was much agitated and still weak. He seated her gently on a sofa wheeled near the fire, and sat by her.

"I am your friend," he said, still holding one of

13

her slender hands. "I am always your friend. You are the only woman in the world to me."

There was a long silence. During it, Wilmer gently lifted the hand he held, kissed it, and relinquished it. Then he rose, and walked away to the window, where he stood awhile in a tumult of emotion, striving to reflect, to decide how best to proceed in order to make Drosée perceive him to be patient, and resolved to do her will. Amid his determination to be to her only what it should please her to have him be, mingled a wild, irresistible hope that she would and did love him, and a desire at once passionate and full of reverence to claim all he could, even now. Joy and pain were so mixed in this suspense that he cou'd scarcely tell which predominated; but he meant above everything that Drosée should not be pained or agitated by his own feelings.

"Mr. Wilmer!" said her soft, low voice.

He returned to her side instantly.

"I have just learned that you saved my life," she said.

"I wish it were so," he answered; "I bungled horribly in trying to do it. I cannot bear to remember that night."

"I have heard what you did," she said ; "I owe my life to you."

"And I owe all my happiness to your promised friendship," he said. "I have never told you, Miss Alwyn, with what a feeling you have inspired me. I think I never can. It is confidence, such as I have never before felt in any living soul. No honor any human being could confer upon me could make me so proud and so happy as the name, from you, of friend."

A little pain shot through Drosée's doubting heart. Was it then friendship after all? She looked up. The soft trouble in her eyes sent a swift intoxication through his veins. His heart began to throb quickly, and his look grew more intense. Her eyelashes trembled, but did not fall. They looked each other in the eyes, silently reading each other's thoughts. Slowly Drosée's cheek flushed ; slowly a smile of the tenderest, most joyful triumph lit his dark and ardent face ; he bent forward, and breathed, rather than spoke to her :

"Love, will you trust all to me ?"

She sunk away from him a little, closing her eyes, but putting out her hands to him. He took and held them fast. His face, ardent, brilliant, and glorious with happiness, was near her own; but he did not offer to approach nearer. She needed time, and he gave it her, restraining his own impetuous delight for her sweet sake. His reward came duly. She opened her eyes, and glanced up with a trusting, confiding, tender look.

"You are so gentle, and so true, and so wise," she said, softly. "I trust you."

They were silent, then, for a moment's space; and then Louis and Jo were heard returning.

"You are all in the dark!" said Jo's fresh voice, as she came in, her cheeks aglow from the crisp air.

"Good evening, Miss Jo," said Wilmer's deep voice, serenely.

"Who are you?" Jo asked, puzzled. Then, as Louis struck a match and lit the gas, she extended to him a cordial little hand.

"You are here, are you? We have been to the hotel to ask you to come. Dr. Stark will be here tonight."

Louis and Wilmer shook hands.

"It is splendid out of doors, Drosée," Louis said. "I met the doctor, and I told him if to-morrow was fine I was going to take you out."

"With the doctor's permission," Wilmer said promptly, looking at Drosée—"I have Miss Alwyn's, I believe?—I am going to bring a sleigh here for her to-morrow morning."

Louis nodded. "You have been making good use of your twilight hour," he thought to himself.

Mrs. Johns came bustling in, now, welcomed Wilmer, and invited the whole party in to supper. Dr. Stark arrived soon after they had all returned to the parlor. He noticed when he came in that Wilmer and Drosée were talking a little apart, and from his friend's alternate fits of abstraction and brilliancy during the evening's conversation drew his own conclusions.

"I must deliver a request," he said to Drosée, before going, having secured her to himself for a while. "Mr. Bell walked part of the way with me this evening. He has been very assiduous in his attentions to me lately, in order, I gather, to hear from you, my friend. To-night, learning that I was coming here, he asked me to request that you would receive him to-morrow, if convenient. Do you know what a hopeless flame he cherishes for you, child? He is like all the rest of us, yours to command."

"I cannot see him to-morrow," Drosée answered. "Mr. Wilmer is going to stay, and take me out, if it is fine weather."

"Sits the wind so? Nay, Penserosa, do not let me make you blush! I am an old, old friend; I am happy in your happiness; the life you are suited for is opening to you—a fair and liberal life, full of the rare strength and joy of a well-chosen companionship. It is—I say it reverently, my good child—of such stuff as you that wives and mothers are made who help the world 'move sunward!'"

Wilmer did not guess what made Drosée's fair face glow with such a fine, faint flame as he came to her side immediately after this, when Dr. Stark had made his adieux; but after he had followed his friend with a simple hand-clasp and gone out into the night, he still remembered the new-lit radiance of the gentle eyes looking trustfully up to his as he bade good-night.

The lovers took a short, delightful drive next

morning over the hard, fine snow, packed by weeks of sleighing.

"It is late in February, and we are still buried in snow," Drosée said, as they drew near home.

"Yes, we are in the snow, but spring is coming!" Wilmer said, in a low, vibrating voice; and he looked at Drosée with a subdued, but penetrating, gladness in his whole expression.

They had been talking to each other as no lovers, unless also true friends, can talk; reflection, experience, fact and fancy entered into their conversation and their confidences. That happiness was so fully her own at last Drosée could scarcely realize. She had come back to life with experience and memory to arm her for its strife; and now love itself stood beside her with its divine encouragement!

"You are better for your drive," Wilmer said, as they sat together alone before the fire. He leaned toward her, smiling. Her cheek had a faint, clear rose tint on it, the harbinger of returning health. He cautiously took up the little hand he scarcely, as yet, felt free to touch at will.

Drosée turned her head and looked down into his

face.   The rapt, transfigured look it wore moved her to her heart's depths.

"You are very happy!" she half asked, half exclaimed.   Her voice trembled.

He laughed low with delight, and gently clasped her in one arm.   Leaning closer, he lightly, half-timidly, kissed her cheek.

"I am very happy!" he said, whispering.

At this first near caress a slow fire kindled on Drosée's cheek.   She quivered slightly, and he drew her closer to him.

"I will make you happy, my darling," he said, softly.

"You will help me to do right and to live aright," she said, as softly.

Then he bowed his head reverently, his eyes looking into hers; they kissed each other; and life began again with a new and sacred joy.

THE END.

LAST DAYS OF
KNICKERBOCKER LIFE IN NEW YORK.

By ABRAM C. DAYTON.

"The reading of this unpretending little volume is as pleasant as a long chat with an old friend in an afternoon of summer."—*N. Y. Tribune.*

"An instructing, entertaining volume."—*N. Y. Herald.*

"A genial book, overflowing with pleasant and instructive chat concerning New York, its inhabitants, and its institutions in 1831. Will prove highly interesting to the general reader."—*Chronicle Herald, Philadelphia.*

"We have been able to offer but random glimpses of this interesting book, which is really a magazine of local anecdote and reminiscence."—*N. Y. Sun.*

"A lively, mellow volume of remembrances of old New York, written in familiar chit-chat style."—*Public Ledger, Philadelphia.*

"Bright, cheery, and gossipy."—*Chicago Evening Journal.*

"Charming reminiscences of New York forty years ago. The book speaks to us like an old friend, and we lay it down with regret."—*Boston Courier.*

"The author was a vivacious, entertaining man, a witness of the scenes he describes, and thousands of readers will be intensely interested in these pages."—*N. Y. Observer.*

1 vol., cloth, 16mo, $1 25.

Henry Wadsworth Longfellow:

A MEDLEY IN PROSE AND VERSE.

BY RICHARD HENRY STODDARD.

A brilliant volume of reminiscences. Includes the recollections of a number of literary celebrities, among others Dr. T. M. Coan, Felix Adler, R. Swain Gifford, and Julian Hawthorne. An artistic steel-plate portrait of the deceased poet, from a photograph by Sarony, accompanies the volume. One of the most elegant tributes to the beloved poet, in book form, that this year will witness. The names of author and contributors to this book would of themselves be a sufficient guarantee of the authenticity of facts narrated, but it has not been deemed amiss to embody a letter touching on this point from the poet himself.

1 vol., cloth, large octavo, $1 50.

The Skeleton in the House:

A NOVELETTE.

FROM THE GERMAN OF

FRIEDRICH SPIELHAGEN
By MARY J. SAFFORD.

"A novelette with as much plot and movement as a piece for the theatre. Spielhagen at his best."—*N. Y. Daily Times.*

"As good as a play. It is a piece of clever mystification, which introduces us to the household of one of the great northern merchant-princes."—*The Nation.*

"The most original piece of comical extravagance that has appeared for a long time. The grim title is a piece of solemn mystification, and the reader is played with till at last he hardly knows whether he is reading farce or tragedy."—*The Graphic,* London.

Price, in Paper, 25 Cents.